'**Scott McPherson is the new orthopaedic registrar.**'

'Not *the* Scott McPherson!' Heather exclaimed.

'Yes.'

'Oh-h-h,' she groaned, biting her bottom lip. She had never been able to banish Scott from her mind since the accident. His face kept popping up every time she saw a broken leg. 'Of all the orthopaedic registrars in the country, why did he have to come to my unit?'

Then her face brightened. 'Perhaps he won't remember me,' Heather said hopefully.

Patricia Robertson has nursed in hospitals, in District Health, and abroad. Now retired, she is incorporating this past experience in her Medical Romances. Widowed with two daughters, her hobbies are gardening, reading, and taking care of her Yorkshire terriers. She lives in Scotland.

HEALING THE BREAK

BY
PATRICIA ROBERTSON

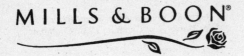

MILLS & BOON®

*First published in Great Britain 1998
Harlequin Mills & Boon Limited,
Eton House, 18-24 Paradise Road, Richmond, Surrey TW9 1SR*

© Patricia Robertson 1998

ISBN 0 263 80519 0

*Set in Times 10 on 12 pt. by
Rowland Phototypesetting Limited
Bury St Edmunds, Suffolk*

03-9801-44391-D

*Printed and bound in Great Britain
by Mackays of Chatham PLC, Chatham*

CHAPTER ONE

TEARS mixed with the rain on Heather's cheeks as she rushed from Bill's flat. How had she not realised that he was seeing someone else? Love must have blinded her. Apparently he had met this other woman soon after they had become engaged. Why hadn't he told her then— the rat?

She remembered now the funny looks some of her nursing colleagues had given her, and the sudden silences as she had approached. At the time it had not penetrated her thick skull that they had been talking about her, lost as she had been in a haze of love. Her cheeks burned as she realised what an idiot she had been.

As she pulled her anorak about her she found that in her haste she had snatched up Bill's. It was too big for her and smelled of him, but as it was raining she didn't give in to her first impulse—which was to tear it off.

Wrapped in her distress, she stepped off the pavement without looking. It was the skid of the motorbike on the wet road which jerked her back to reality.

Horror held her immobile for several seconds as she realised that she was responsible for the accident which had just happened. The whirling of one of the bike's wheels was the only sound to disturb the silence of the suburban road. Most of the occupants of the flats were at work and any children were at school.

A groan from the sprawled figure unfroze her and she

rushed forward, reaching him just as he pulled off his helmet.

'You shouldn't have done that.' Her anxiety made her snap as she knelt beside him. My, he was big, six feet at least, her mind registered, and broadly built. She'd never be able to lift him.

'I'm an orthopaedic doctor and it's my leg that's broken not my neck, though I'd like to wring yours,' he said angrily, through teeth clenched with pain.

'Yes, I expect you would.' She tried to sound soothing in spite of her distress. 'But does anything else hurt?' she asked, her hands stretched forward to feel his limbs.

'No, everything's in good working order except my leg,' he said grittily, pushing her hands away and wondering if this was a bag lady who was crouching over him in a too-big anorak. She had dropped a bulging plastic bag beside him.

'If you say so,' she said shortly, stung by his retort. She'd only been concerned for him, after all.

His leather jacket and black trousers were muddied and soaked by the wet road. His short black hair was damp and clung to his skull, making him look vulnerable, and she forgot her distress

She slipped off Bill's anorak, covered him with it and wiped a stray hair from his forehead, looking at him compassionately.

'It'll get ruined,' he told her gruffly, impressed by her kindness in spite of himself and realising that his first impression had been mistaken. This was no bag lady, even though she looked as if her clothes had come from a jumble sale. The bright pink cardigan was certainly not in fashion.

'It's the least I can do,' she said, feeling even more

guilty that he should think of her at such a time. 'I'll go and phone for an ambulance.' Fortunately there was a phone box nearby—she only hoped it hadn't been vandalised.

As she made to rise he caught hold of her arm in a surprisingly strong grip. 'If you really want to do something for me. . .' She was held back as much by the urgency in his tone as by his restraining hand. 'You can take this. . .' He struggled to pull an envelope out of his trouser pocket. As Heather strove to help him it tore as the rain dampened it.

'You're a menace to society,' he said in a disbelieving voice. He gave a big irritated sigh. 'Phone the number at the top of the letterhead and tell them Scott McPherson can't come for the interview.'

As she took it from him he groaned and his blue eyes filled with pain.

Feeling even more miserable, she said, 'I'll do it when the ambulance has arrived.'

'No, now.' His voice was authoritative.

'No, I won't leave you,' she said firmly. 'I'll do it when the ambulance is here,' she repeated, and rushed away to make her phone call before he could raise further objections.

Returning to him, she drew a tissue from her plastic bag. He was in too much pain to object as she wiped his face gently with it. He would have liked to have remonstrated when she took off that ghastly cardigan to put under his head and when she took his large hand in her small warm one but, in spite of his anger against her, there was something comforting about her. He was in so much pain that he just gave up and closed his eyes.

The rain must have stopped, he decided, for he couldn't

feel it. He then opened his eyes—to find a duck, staring him in the face. He must be delirious, he decided, then realised it was the handle of the umbrella this woman was holding over him.

'The ambulance is almost here,' she said reassuringly. 'You can hear its siren.'

A few people suddenly appeared, drawn by the siren. 'Please phone that number and explain,' Scott begged a few minutes later as the paramedics gently rendered first aid and put him on a stretcher.

'But wouldn't it be better if I came with you?' she asked as she walked beside the stretcher.

'No, it definitely would not,' he said adamantly, his brows drawn together in a frown which was not altogether due to his pain. 'Just do as I ask,' he added wearily.

Heather had been too concerned about Scott to notice the police arrive. She was watching the ambulance move away when the sergeant said, 'I'd like some details of the accident.' He was a fatherly man with kind eyes.

Perhaps they sent him to interview accident cases, Heather thought inconsequentially. 'It was my fault,' she admitted. 'I walked into the road without looking.' Distress at having caused the accident—and the reason for it—made her eyes fill with tears. 'You see, my fiancé had just broken off our engagement.' It was said not as an excuse but in a heartfelt way.

The grey-haired police sergeant patted her arm. 'I'm sorry,' he said sympathetically, 'but I ought to warn you that you might be sued.'

'Oh-h-h!' Heather groaned, her shoulders sagging.

The policeman drew out his pencil and notebook and Heather gave him the details. 'Will you be able to get home OK?' he asked solicitously as he finished questioning her.

'Yes, thanks.' She gave him a tremulous smile.

He drove away and she was left alone, the few onlookers having dispersed as soon as the ambulance had left.

Heather straightened her shoulders and went to the phone box. Once inside, she searched in her plastic bag for her purse and drew out the required coins.

Wearily she opened the letter, to discover that the man's interview had been for an orthopaedic consultant's post. She almost dropped it in horror for she knew how scarce these posts were.

She was the cause of him missing this chance and it was almost too much to bear, as was the fact that he would have been given the post. Of this she had no doubt. Even in pain, Scott McPherson had a 'presence'. She dialled the number and left the message.

It was a bedraggled Heather who turned the key in the door of her flat shortly afterwards. Thank goodness her flatmate was on holiday. She needed to be alone.

That evening she phoned the hospital to find out how Scott was. She was told that he was 'comfortable', the stock word which meant that he was all right. She enquired about visiting times, knowing she would have to steel herself to see him to apologise once more—and find out if he planned to sue her.

Heather spent a miserable, wakeful night and was glad to rise. She wished she had the early shift as concentrating on her work would have kept her distress at bay.

Her flat was close to the London hospital where she was a junior staff nurse on Female Medical. As she made her way to work later she thought, Well at least I won't have a constant reminder of the damage I've done to that poor man as I would have had on an orthopaedic ward.

In a way, this thought was tinged with regret because she was interested in orthopaedics and had decided to specialise in this field before the accident. But now. . .?

Bill was a doctor at the same hospital. The grapevine had spread the news of their broken engagement by the time she reported for duty. As she was a popular girl colleagues kept stopping her to commiserate. While their sympathy was acceptable it made the pain worse.

The only good thing about the accident was that it deflected her thoughts away from her lost love to some extent.

Heather phoned Scott's hospital every day to enquire how he was. She allowed three days for him to recover from his operation and shock, then went to see him.

It had been one of the wettest summers on record, and it was raining again on the July afternoon Heather entered the hospital.

Scott had been admitted to a private ward. As she made her way there Heather wondered apprehensively if he would see her. Perhaps she should ask the sister to find out first.

On reaching the floor, Heather gave her name and explained her position to the sister, who readily agreed to ask Scott if she could see him.

'Yes, he'll see you, Miss Langley,' the attractive blonde sister said sympathetically, and showed her the way.

Heather's firm knock on the door hid her trembling insides. She entered at his bidding, thinking to herself,

What a pleasant voice he has—I only hope it remains that way.

Scott was in bed, wearing blue pyjamas which emphasised the blueness of his eyes. What beautiful eyes, she thought. Pity their expression is so grim. He was definitely not amused to see her.

Her heart fluttered with anxiety. He looked almost like a different man from the one who had lain wet and muddy in the road. His short black hair was neatly combed and the rest of him was spotlessly clean. Only the lines of pain at the corners of his eyes were the same.

Heather's heart filled with compassion when she noted the gauntness of his face. I'm responsible for that, she thought guiltily.

Scott had almost refused to see her, but he remembered her kindness and was curious to hear what she would say. 'So you've come to apologise,' he said, less sternly than he'd intended.

She wasn't as he'd remembered her, either. Her red hair, which had been darkened by the rain and plastered to her head, was shining and brightened the gloomy daylight in the room. She was wearing clean blue jeans and a navy blue anorak and looked sparkling. The anxiety in her eyes was the same, though.

Heather straightened shoulders which threatened to droop. 'Yes,' she said, pleased to hear the firmness of her tone. 'I'm very sorry and—' She rushed on to add, 'I wouldn't blame you if you wanted to sue me, but I have to tell you I've only a hundred pounds in the bank.' She sat down abruptly on the chair which had been placed at his bedside, clutched the flowers she'd brought to her chest and looked at him apprehensively.

The honesty of her admission about her financial state

he found amusing, but it was her vulnerable expression which softened him. 'So the police didn't contact you?' he asked gently.

'Again? No,' she said, becoming more apprehensive. 'I told them it was my fault. Are they planning to bring an action as well?'

'No,' he said evenly. 'They told me the reason for your jay-walking.'

'Oh, they had no right,' Heather said sharply, tears close to the surface.

'Perhaps not,' he said firmly. He really must not let the closeness of her tears sway him. She had, after all, been the cause of him fracturing his femur and possibly losing the chance of a consultancy. 'But it saved your bacon, didn't it?'

Hanging onto the shreds of her courage, she rose to her feet and looked him straight in the eye. 'I don't want your sympathy to influence you,' she said, taking refuge in sarcasm so he wouldn't see her distress. 'Go ahead and sue.' Her eyes were sparkling with fire as she turned to leave.

She had her hand on the door when he said in a bland tone, 'Are those flowers for me?'

Heather swung round and held them out, then realised that in her distress she had hugged them to her and they were in tatters.

With dignity she laid them gently on the bed. 'Yes,' she said, her chin up.

Scott hid his amusement behind a cool, 'Thank you. I'll accept them instead of bringing an action against you.'

'Thank you,' she said, with her dignity intact.

As she left the room she frowned. Had he been laughing at her? Shaking her head, she thought, What does it matter? I'm never going to see him again.

Heather found the next three months trying. She seemed to be constantly bumping into Bill. When her brother, Gavin, phoned to tell her there was a vacancy for a staff nurse on the orthopaedic ward at Waverly General, where he was a junior doctor, her interest in orthopaedics returned.

It would be great to join him, especially as he'd offered to share his flat with her. She was half-Scottish and loved Edinburgh so she decided to apply.

It was just what she needed—a complete change.

CHAPTER TWO

'DO YOU know what I heard today?' Gavin Langley asked.

'No,' Heather replied absent-mindedly. She was at the decreasing end of the pterodactyl she was knitting. Although she had a row tally, her mind did wander and she sometimes forgot to use it. This time she was concentrating hard on the small wings so that they would both be the same size. In the past some had been lopsided.

'Scott McPherson is the new orthopaedic registrar,' Gavin told her.

'What did you say?' Heather was frowning at the row tally. Surely she hadn't missed adding a stitch?

'Scott McPherson is the new orthopaedic registrar,' Gavin repeated loudly.

This time she did hear him and raised horror-stricken hazel eyes to her brother's blues ones—they're the same colour as Scott's, she thought—and dropped a stitch. 'Not *the* Scott McPherson!' Her face paled.

'Yes.'

'Oh-h-h,' she groaned, biting her bottom lip. She had never been able to banish Scott from her mind since the accident. His face kept popping up every time she saw a broken leg. 'Of all the orthopaedic registrars in the country, why did he have to come to my unit?'

She put the needles together and shoved them viciously into the ball of wool, forgetting to pick up the stitch. Then her face brightened.

'Perhaps he won't remember me,' she said, looking hopefully across at her brother, who was standing watching a couple of young boys skating precariously on roller blades on the pavement beneath their flat.

Gavin turned to face her. 'He's hardly likely to forget the person who fractured his femur,' he said wryly, his dark eyebrows rising.

He was two years older than Heather and built like a rugby player, six feet two, broad and muscular with a rugged face. Gavin was a houseman on the medical unit at Waverly General.

Heather crossed the room to join her brother and looked up at him, unaware of the sadness in her eyes. 'I'd hoped I'd put all that behind me when I came up here.' Mention of Scott had brought back the pain of her break with Bill.

Gavin's face became more serious. He had forgotten about Heather's broken engagement, but the flash of sadness in her eyes had reminded him.

Putting an arm around her shoulder, he led her to the couch and pulled her down beside him. 'Your hair's short now.' He ruffled the short red curls affectionately. 'And it was sixteen months ago and in London. He'll never connect you with it here in Edinburgh.'

'You are a darling,' she said as she looked up at him with troubled eyes, guilt over the accident still haunting her.

'Look, don't distress yourself. He didn't know you were a nurse.' Gavin's easygoing face smiled.

'That's right, no, he didn't.' The tense lines on her face relaxed.

He gave her a hug. 'You'd better finish that pterodactyl—it won't be able to fly with uneven wings.' He laughed.

Monday came all too soon. Waverly General was an old hospital, set in the heart of Edinburgh. The orthopaedic unit was small, consisting of just a male and female ward which could be reached by a walkway as well as through the corridors. The main orthopaedic hospital was on the outskirts of Edinburgh.

Heather usually walked through the corridors of the hospital, with their tiled walls, to enter the unit that way. She liked to imagine that she'd been swept back in time to when nurses in old-fashioned uniforms, doctors in frock coats and beards and patients dressed in Victorian garb had walked this way.

What was it like then? she mused. They hadn't had the pain control they had today or the anaesthesia. Heather shivered as she imagined the cries of pain that must have come from the wards.

As she turned into the corridor which led to the ortho-paedic unit she straightened her uniform, wishing the colour suited her more. The dark turquoise, she always felt, made her look flamboyant with her red hair. Never mind, she comforted herself, the sisters wore white and that's what she would be wearing if her ambitions materialised.

'You're late, Staff Nurse Langley,' Charge Nurse Peter McLean barked as Heather entered the office.

She glanced at her watch. It was exactly seven o'clock. 'I'm dead on time,' she said, a restless night making her sound aggrieved.

'Got you that time,' Peter said with a grin.

Heather smiled back. Peter was an excellent ward

'sister', but he did like his little joke and usually at one of the staff's expense.

The other nurses laughed. 'That's what I like to see.' Peter's round face beamed. 'A cheerful beginning to the day. Right, Maggie,' he spoke to the night staff nurse. 'Let's see what damage you've managed to do.'

'Not much, I hope,' Maggie said, looking at him tiredly. 'We have a new patient in the side-ward. An amputee.' Her eyes were compassionate as she continued, 'A young man of twenty-six, Alan McDermott. He was in a car accident and was operated on last night.'

It was like a painting—the nurses in their pale turquoise uniforms, a contrast to Heather's darker shade which denoted her status, grouped about Peter who wore tunic and trousers, his blue charge nurse shoulder-flashes breaking the whiteness of his uniform.

He was sitting at the desk with the night nurse, bending over to read the report. A shaft of early morning light caught and held them for a moment. Maggie's voice was the only sound that disturbed the stillness. Then the picture disintegrated as the report finished and the night staff left.

'We expect a new registrar, Scott McPherson, to be on the round this morning,' Peter told them. 'He's come from a London hospital so we must be extra careful to show him that our standards are as good as, if not better than, those he may have been used to.'

Peter's brown eyes fixed on each of them as he spoke. They had seen that expression before and their previous smiles vanished. 'Yes, Peter,' they said in unison. They knew his bark was worse than his bite, but they also knew how serious he was about his profession.

'Good.' He rose to his six-foot height, taller than the

three female nurses but the same height as David Curtiss—the only other male nurse. 'Right. You special Alan McDermott in the side-ward today, David,' Peter told him. 'And the rest of you, breakfasts then bedpan and back care.' He clapped his hands lightly. 'Off you go, and remember I expect a spotless ward by ten o'clock.' He put his hand on Heather's arm. 'You stay, Staff.'

When the others had left Peter said, 'Supervise the ward for me, will you, Heather, while I make sure the notes are up to date? I've heard a rumour that our new registrar can be a stickler.'

Heather wasn't surprised to hear this, remembering Scott's 'presence', and apprehension caught her afresh. 'Right.'

She was about to leave the office when Peter glanced up from the treatment book. 'I want to check on Michael's back before the round. The report said it was quite red.' Peter sighed. 'He was probably itchy and swivelled around on it. It only takes a crumb.'

Heather nodded. 'Did the occupational therapist think of anything new to keep him from being bored?' she asked.

'Not really,' he told her. 'Anything she suggested was greeted with derision, and a "That's for old people" when she suggested basket-making.'

'I'm sorry for him,' Heather said, sympathy showing in her eyes. 'It must be tough to be nineteen and confined to bed, strung up in traction, for about three months.'

'He should have thought of that before riding too fast on a wet road. No wonder his motorbike skidded and he fractured his femur.' Peter's face was stern. 'It's just luck no one else was hurt.'

'You're right,' Heather said, the conversation bringing back to mind that other accident. Would Scott McPherson remember her? she wondered. She couldn't comfort herself that Scott had been speeding.

'Sorry to inflict you with my hobby-horse,' Peter said, his Glasgow accent becoming stronger with the force of his emotions, 'but we see too many accidents here which could have been avoided.'

'So we do,' she agreed. 'Do you want me to do the temperatures?'

'Yes, please.' He handed her the book.

Heather went into the ward. There were twenty-four beds in all, twelve lined on either side. The walls were a pale shade of green, and curtains in a dark and pale green striped material hung beside each bed. They provided privacy when the doctors wanted to examine patients or treatments were to be carried out.

At the bottom of the ward there was a convalescent room where those who were able watched television. The sluice was on the left at that end and the shower and toilets to the right. No smoking was allowed.

The clatter of crockery, the crisp noise of cereals being poured into bowls, the smell of toast and the sound of milk and tea filling cups greeted Heather. Breakfasts were in full swing.

The nurses' station was halfway down the left hand side. Michael Grant's bed was directly opposite.

'Hi, Staff,' he called as Heather put the TPR book down on the desk.

Heather smiled and went across to him. A skeletal traction frame made him look as if he had been caught in a cat's cradle.

'I hear the occupational therapist couldn't suggest

something new to do with you,' she said, removing his breakfast tray.

'She wasn't my type,' he quipped. 'Now you. . .' He grinned at her cheekily, a faint pinkness staining his fair skin. His implication was clear.

'Now, then, Mr Grant,' Heather said firmly. He was a very likeable lad and she didn't want to give him a hard put-down, but male patients who were in for some time could become cheeky and needed to be handled carefully but firmly. She had found that using a surname instead of a first name usually showed them where the line was to be drawn.

'Sorry, Staff,' Michael said, blushing. 'I was only having a bit of fun.'

'I know, Michael,' She smiled. 'Why don't you think of something you would really like to do—something you may have thought of in the past but forgotten?'

His hair was as red as her own and he could have been mistaken for her brother. He was certainly more like her than Gavin was. 'I'll give it a go,' he said.

'Did your parents manage to come at the weekend?' Michael came from Skye, and his accident had occurred when he'd been on his way to Edinburgh for an interview at the university. Heather remembered how his admission had reminded her of Scott yet again.

'No.' He tried to hide his disappointment, but it was there in his eyes. 'They're busy on the farm just now and couldn't leave.'

'I can understand that,' Heather said sympathetically. 'My father's a farmer, too.'

'Where?' Interest glowed in Michael's eyes.

'The Lake District.'

'Whereabouts?'

Heather knew that if she didn't end the conversation now Michael would keep her talking. It was one of his ploys to alleviate his boredom.

'Keswick way,' she said, adding, 'I must go, Michael. Charge Nurse will be coming to take a look at your back later.'

'Staff.' The anxious tone of his voice held her back.

'Yes?' She gave him an encouraging look.

'It's about my back.' He looked embarrassed.

'Yes, what about it?' Heather could not understand why he was looking so guilty.

'It's my fault it's sore.'

'How?'

'She won't get into trouble, will she?' He looked as if he wished he hadn't spoken.

'Who?' Heather frowned in puzzlement.

'Nurse Patterson.'

'Why should she get into trouble?' Heather was becoming suspicious.

'I had a bedpan in the night and. . .' his embarrassment deepened '. . .the fleece got marked. She took it away and forgot to give me a clean one.'

Heather frowned. Looking after patients' pressure areas was most important, especially for someone like Michael who was virtually tied to the bed. 'And you didn't remind her?'

'Well, that accident case came in just then and they were so busy I thought it could wait until the day staff came on.' He shrugged. 'You won't tell the charge nurse, will you?'

'Well, that will depend on how bad your back is,' she said, not able to promise. Broken skin took a long time to heal.

'It's not bad,' he assured her.

'Hmm, I'll get you a sheepskin.' She hurried away, returning immediately with a bowl of warm water and the sheepskin.

She pulled the curtains round the bed. 'I'll just wash your back first. Up you go.' Michael was in sliding traction that allowed him some movement.

Heather had a quick look at his buttocks. There was a small red area on his left one. She inspected the sheet for crumbs but there were none so she took the cloth used for his back and gave the area a gentle wash, dried it well and then slipped the sheepskin in quickly. 'OK, lower away,' she said, smiling to soften the anxiety in the young man's eyes.

'Not too bad?' he asked, relieved.

'Could be worse,' she said.

'You won't tell Charge Nurse, will you?'

'We'll see what it's like later and if it's OK I'll ask Night Staff to mention it to Nurse Patterson.'

'Thanks.'

It was obvious that Michael had a crush on Sandra Patterson, who was new to the ward and about his own age.

Heather checked the skin close to the Steinmann's pin which had been inserted through the neck of his tibia for a Bohler's stirrup to be clamped onto it. 'Well, this looks fine. Nice and clean.'

'Yes,' Michael said. 'Nurse Patterson cleaned the skin last night before I went to sleep as it was a bit itchy,' he said sheepishly.

'I'm glad to hear that.' Heather went to the bottom of the bed to check the weights. 'We must keep the traction right to reduce your fractured femur, as you very well know.'

Michael laughed. 'I'm becoming an expert.'

Peter was going round the patients, asking them how they were and listening carefully to their replies. Heather knew how important it was, this listening, but it had to be genuine. The patients sensed if it wasn't. Heather was always careful when a patient was telling her a long story about his family. In it somewhere she would find what was distressing him. It was as much a part of nursing as the more practical side.

The breakfasts were cleared away, the bedpan round was completed and the ward tidied.

Peter beckoned to her just as she was about to take the temperatures. He was pulling the curtains round Michael's bed. 'Come and have a look at Michael's back with me before the round.'

Michael looked at her apprehensively. She didn't mention she had already seen it, and patted Michael on the shoulder reassuringly.

'Let's have a look at your back,' Peter said and Michael obliged. 'It's only a bit pink,' Peter told him and Michael sighed with relief. Even that short time on the sheepskin had relieved the redness a little.

'Were you worried?' Peter had heard the sigh and was looking at him sympathetically.

'I think he was worried you would tell him off,' Heather said blithely.

'And so I should,' Peter said sternly, but his eyes smiled. 'See that you don't let any more crumbs leap off your plate.' He grinned.

'I'll do my best,' Michael promised.

Once Michael had been made comfortable Heather

took the temperatures, then did the medicine round with one of the nurses.

'Staff, will I really be going home today?' Trevor Cameron asked her as she speeded up the ward with a covered urinal which she had found under a bed.

'Yes, Mr Cameron,' she told him, pausing beside the chair in which he was sitting. 'Mr Blacklock said you could. We've arranged for a home help to come twice a week.'

'I can manage without that,' he said, his lined face stiffening. 'And my daughter-in-law is very good.'

Trevor Cameron had fallen in his flat and fractured the neck of his femur, which had been pinned successfully.

He was an active seventy-year-old and insisted on living on his own. He was fiercely independent, and had blue eyes which reminded Heather of another pair of blue eyes. Oh, dear, she thought nervously, Scott will be here any moment.

'Your daughter-in-law's having a baby and it's her fourth,' Heather said kindly. 'She's bound to be a bit tired.' Sarah Cameron had looked worn out when she'd visited yesterday. 'I know you'll want to help her all you can,' Heather smiled encouragingly.

'I suppose you're right,' he agreed reluctantly, 'but I don't like strangers in the house.' He sounded petulant.

'She won't be a stranger for long,' Heather told him cheerfully. 'And it'll be someone else for you to talk to until you can get about more.'

'Oh, yes.' Trevor brightened. He hadn't thought of that.

She smiled and hurried to the sluice.

Much as she would have liked to delay her meeting with Scott, Heather hoped her chat with Mr Cameron hadn't made her late for the ward round. It would only bring attention to her.

She washed her hands and walked quickly up the ward. 'Wouldn't do to be late for the round today, Staff,' Michael said with a grin, putting into words what she had been thinking.

She grimaced at him and hurried on.

When Heather reached the office she had to stifle a groan. They were all there—Will Mackenzie, the houseman, Scott McPherson and Thomas Blacklock, the consultant, who was just saying, 'I expect you'll think it old-fashioned, Scott, that I've put Michael Grant in traction but I felt it would be better for his comminuted fracture.' It was a statement and there was no apology in it.

As Scott just nodded Heather suspected he would have treated Michael's fractured femur differently.

Her arrival drew his eyes to her. He was standing with the light from the window full on his face, and he was big—bigger than she remembered.

Was her heart beating faster with anxiety or because she'd suddenly realised how attractive he was? The last time she'd seen him he'd been gaunt, with pain lines making him look older.

Now he was wearing a white shirt which would have made a good advertisement for a soap powder, a university tie, dark grey trousers and the doctor's badge of office, the white coat, which he wore with ease and assurance.

She was doing the very thing she particularly didn't want to—drawing attention to herself by staring at him.

He really was handsome. It wasn't just his blue eyes, his square-jawed face, his dark, almost black wavy hair, his six-foot height and his nicely put together figure. It was something else. There was a depth to him which some extremely handsome people lacked. Here was a man who would not disappoint you. There was integrity in the way he held himself, confidence in his assured gaze.

He smiled with amusement as he saw her staring at him, and his smile made him even more attractive. Heather steeled herself. Men were not on her agenda at the moment—this man in particular.

Scott frowned slightly. 'Have we met before?' he asked.

The last time Heather had heard his voice she hadn't noticed his soft Edinburgh accent. It was like a caress, but his words were not. Her face tightened with anxiety.

Before she could answer Peter said, smiling at Heather, 'Let me introduce you, Mr McPherson. This is Staff Nurse Heather Langley, the best staff nurse we have.'

It wasn't her name that reminded Scott that here was the woman who had been the cause of his accident and him losing the chance of a consultant's post. It was the look of anxiety he remembered.

His face darkened. It was as if winter had suddenly swept summer aside. 'I remember now,' he said, and even his voice seemed to have hardened. 'We *have* met before.'

CHAPTER THREE

'You can renew your acquaintance later, Scott,' Thomas Blacklock said brusquely. Small of build, round of face, balding with grey hair and dapperly dressed, he reminded Heather of a bank manager. His eyes redeemed the fussy, dogmatic impression he gave. They were blue, intelligent, and could soften with a kindness he strove to conceal. 'We'll leave last night's accident case till last,' he said.

'Yes, sir,' Scott said evenly, not at all put out.

Heather wanted to hang back, but as she was in the doorway and Peter was pushing the trolley with the case notes towards her she had to help. She went into the corridor and opened the ward door, Scott stepping forward to push the other one back.

Now was her chance to bring up the rear but, after the others had passed through, Scott gestured for her to precede him. 'After you, Staff,' he said with an expressionless face.

Heather could feel his presence behind her as they caught up with the others, and quickened her step. As he drew level she glanced up at him and saw an ironic twist to his lips, and her heart sank.

It was a pity Mr Blacklock insisted that all the staff went on the round, otherwise she could have slipped away.

The consultant introduced the new registrar to the ward generally before they commenced the round. 'Mr

McPherson will be looking after you,' he told them. 'He's a good orthopaedic man and you can have complete faith in his judgement.'

Here was his kindness showing. He understood how a new face might cause anxiety. Thomas then drew in a quick breath and frowned as if to cover his human lapse.

The round commenced.

Michael grinned at the consultant when they stopped at his bed. He knew all about Thomas Blacklock's kindness for the consultant phoned his parents frequently to keep them up to date with their son's progress. 'Everything all right?' Thomas asked.

'Yes, thank you, sir,' Michael said cheerfully.

They moved forward. I wonder how Scott McPherson will be judged by the patients? Heather thought, glancing at him where he stood too close to her. She couldn't read from his neutral expression what he was thinking.

Thomas stopped at the foot of Ian Ramsay's bed. 'Operation on Wednesday. Don't worry, we'll have you out in time for your wedding.' An infrequent smile lit his features. This was another patient with whom Thomas had concerned himself.

'Thanks, Doctor,' Ian said, his face brightening. He was twenty-five years old and a keen football player. A football accident had torn the cartilage in his left knee joint and the loose gristly fragments were to be removed arthroscopically.

Thomas turned to Scott. 'We don't do a total meniscectomy here,' he said. 'Could lead to osteoarthritis in later life.'

Scott nodded and smiled at the patient, who grinned back. Ian was not a handsome young man, but had lots of personality and an easygoing nature. He taught English at a school in the suburbs and was well liked by the staff and pupils, judging by the number of people who visited him.

The round continued. Discharges were decided upon, with Peter taking notes.

The last patient was Trevor Cameron, who was sitting beside his bed. 'You won't need to see me today,' he said, smiling at the consultant.

'Has Mr Cameron been re-X-rayed?' Thomas asked, looking at Peter.

'No, sir,' Peter told him. 'It wasn't requested.'

'Well, it should have been,' Thomas said brusquely. 'You know I like a check X-ray before my patient goes home. You should have seen to it.'

Peter stiffened at the unfair rebuke, but didn't argue.

Heather's face must have reflected her sympathy at him being reprimanded in front of the patient and staff, especially as the previous registrar was to blame, because Thomas turned to her and said, 'No need for you to look like that, miss. The nursing staff are here to remind the surgeons.'

Heather was furious. 'I thought they were here to take expert care of the patients, sir,' she said tersely, 'not the doctors.'

Oh-h-h! she groaned to herself, as the enormity of what she had done in speaking up to a consultant hit her. Well, it was said now. She straightened her back and held her head up.

Heather could see Scott's face behind Thomas's. There was a frown on it.

A silence followed her outburst. Then Thomas, who was a just man, said, 'You're quite right, Staff.' He turned to Peter. 'I apologise.'

'Does this mean I'll have to stay in longer?' Trevor asked, looking worried.

'No. I'll phone the X-ray department and we'll have you X-rayed immediately,' Thomas said gently.

Heather and Scott again held the doors open for the trolley to pass through. 'You got away with that one,' Scott whispered in her ear as the doors swung together behind them, 'but you won't get away with something like that so easily with me.'

Heather glanced up into blue eyes which were not amused. Better not answer back, she thought, but she wasn't going to let him think she was cowed so she gave him a cool look before she preceded him into the office.

Thomas was on the phone to the X-ray department and Will was glancing at notes he had made. Nurse Campbell came in with coffee just as Thomas replaced the receiver.

'As you did the operation, Scott, I think you should see the accident case,' Thomas said as he accepted a steaming mug from Wendy Campbell. 'You'll be overseeing him from now on.'

'All right, sir,' Scott said. 'Black for me, please,' he told an enquiring Wendy.

Overseeing from now on? What did Mr Blacklock mean? wondered Heather anxiously. She soon found out.

'Scott's taking over from me for the next month,' Thomas told them. 'He's eminently capable.' He smiled up at Scott. 'I'm sure he would be a consultant now if he hadn't missed an interview through no fault of his own.'

My fault, thought Heather guiltily.

The news that Thomas was going away was a surprise

to the staff. He hadn't mentioned it last week, nor had the hospital grapevine.

'I have been asked to. . .' here Thomas mentioned an Arab state '. . .to be part of a team to set up a new hospital.' He smiled. 'The offer only came two days ago—that's why we're lucky to have Scott, who has so much experience, to take over.'

He finished his coffee and rose. 'Well, I'll leave you in Mr McPherson's capable hands,' he said, giving them his rare smile. 'Is there anything we haven't covered, Scott?' he asked.

'No, thank you, sir.'

'Right.'

Heather was nearest the door and opened it for the consultant. Thomas nodded his thanks and left.

A silence followed his going. Scott McPherson was an unknown quantity, and the nursing staff and Will Mackenzie would treat him warily until they'd discovered what he was like.

'You girls can go now,' Peter told his nurses.

As they left Scott's hand shot out to grip Heather's arm, holding her back. Panicking, she thought, Surely he's not going to confront me now?

'I'd like Staff to go with us to see Alan McDermott, Charge Nurse,' he said, releasing Heather.

She breathed a silent sigh of relief. A reprieve.

'Yes, sir?' Peter said, using the 'sir' reserved for the consultant. It came easily to his lips because the registrar was such a commanding figure.

Scott had heard the query in Peter's voice and knew why. 'Mr Blacklock told me he likes his male amputees to be nursed by the male staff.'

'Yes,' Peter said. 'He feels it places less strain on the

patient. Thinks a man losing a leg has enough to cope with without feeling embarrassed in front of the female staff.' He held out Alan's notes to the registrar.

'I see.' Scott looked thoughtful. 'Well, as Alan McDermott is my patient I intend to treat him my way,' he said firmly. Heather could see Will Mackenzie's apprehensive face behind Scott. 'I want the female staff to look after him as well as the male staff. I feel it might help him come to terms with his condition more quickly if he's treated normally.'

Peter was looking doubtfully at him. 'I'll take full responsibility,' Scott said. 'Shall we go?' It was more of a statement than a question.

Heather could see that Scott McPherson was a positive, confident man, not used to having his decisions questioned. There didn't appear to be a soft centre that he strove to hide like Thomas Blacklock did. Scott was a straight-from-the-shoulder man. You would know where you were with him, though it might prove uncomfortable.

If Peter had had fair skin he would have blushed, and Heather suspected that he didn't like the new orthopaedic man. The previous registrar had been inefficient and casual, leaving a lot of minor decisions to Peter who had ably executed then.

Scott wouldn't be like that. He would be a hands-on person. She would enjoy working with him if it hadn't been for the accident.

Heather held the door open for him to pass through, but he gestured for her to precede him. It was just a little courtesy but showed what sort of a man he was, thought Heather. He respected people. Heather was impressed. Normally the doctors, except for Will, swept past her.

David Curtiss, the male nurse, turned from checking

the intravenous drip as they came into the side-ward. Scott nodded to him and smiled at Alan, who was lying flat in the bed with a cradle taking the weight of the bedclothes off his stump.

Scott picked up the charts from the bed-side table. He flipped through them, noting the intravenous intake, urinary output, temperature, blood pressure and any comments made by the staff about the patient's progress.

He went to the top of the bed and looked down at Alan. 'Hello, there,' he said, smiling kindly. 'You won't remember me, I expect, but I operated on you last night.'

'If you did I plan to sue you,' Alan said vehemently.

Oh, I hope he doesn't, thought Heather, remembering her own anxiety when she'd thought Scott was going to sue her.

'You're the one who took off my leg.' His voice was rising. 'You shouldn't have done it without asking me.' He was becoming more agitated. 'I didn't sign a consent form.'

Scott's face became serious. 'No, you didn't, but—'

'You had no right,' Alan interrupted, trying to raise himself in the bed.

'You were unconscious and would have bled to death if we hadn't operated immediately,' Scott said quietly but firmly. 'There was no way we could have saved the bottom half of your leg. It was crushed completely.' He didn't tell the stricken man that the operation had been performed at the accident site.

'You should have left me to die,' Alan said in despair.

'I wouldn't have taken you for a quitter, not after what your father told me about you,' Scott said evenly.

'What did he tell you?' Alan asked, interested in spite of himself.

'That you were trapped in a pothole for twenty hours and never gave up hope of rescue.'

'Oh.' Alan seemed to dismiss this. 'That's a bit different.'

'Not so very,' Scott assured him. 'A man can resume a normal life with an artificial limb if he's determined enough and doesn't give up hope.'

'But what woman would want a man with half a leg?' Alan said, holding back tears. 'And don't give me that one about love conquering all.'

'I wasn't going to,' Scott said. He glanced at Heather with a challenge in his eyes. 'Let's ask Staff's opinion.'

Heather resented the challenge. What sort of a person did he think she was? She didn't go round breaking people's legs all the time, nor would she treat anybody, especially a patient, unsympathetically. She hadn't treated Scott like that. He must have forgotten.

Quick to relieve Alan's apprehension, Heather did not look at him sympathetically. Instead, she gave him that look a woman gives a man she finds attractive. A smile twinkled in her eyes as she said, 'I don't think women will notice you have an artificial limb—not when they feel that sex appeal oozing from you.'

They all laughed, even the patient. Heather was certainly not making it up. Alan was a very attractive young man of twenty-six with blond hair and blue eyes.

Scott glanced at her approvingly. He hadn't forgotten her kindness to him—he had just wanted it confirmed.

When Heather realised this she should have resented him checking on her professionalism, but she was pleased by his approval.

'There you are, then,' Scott said as he lifted the bed-clothes covering the cradle to inspect the stump. There was no sign of bleeding through the bandage. Scott glanced again at the chart. 'You seem to be taking fluids well so we'll take down the drip, but you must drink a lot.' Scott noted the tension in Alan's face and knew it wasn't due only to the loss of his leg. 'How's the pain?'

'Not too bad,' Alan said, trying to be brave.

'We'll see you get plenty of relief for that,' Scott told him.

Alan's face relaxed. 'Thanks.'

'You've got a fight ahead of you,' Scott said, looking at him kindly, 'but I know you'll come through OK.' His tone was positive.

Alan gave a tremulous smile. 'Thanks for your confidence.'

Scott patted the young man's shoulder.

They left the side-ward and entered the office, where Scott sat down at the desk, before looking up at Will.

'Alan's family lives in Glasgow so we'll transfer him there when he's recovered sufficiently. Meantime, I want him to be kept pain-free—that way we might be able to reduce his phantom pains.' He swung his glance to Peter.

'There are a couple of drains in the wound so there'll be quite a bit of leakage. You'll be able to remove them in forty-eight hours if the drainage isn't heavy.' He wrote in Alan's notes. 'Reapply the crêpe bandage regularly to maintain adequate compression to keep the oedema down. We can change it for an Elset sock eventually.'

He looked up at the charge nurse again. Peter's face was stiff with resentment at being told how to look after an amputee.

'I know you have a lot of experience,' Scott said quietly, 'but my ways may be different to Mr Blacklock's and I don't want any misunderstandings.' His tone was firm. 'So we'll keep the patient flat at all times to prevent flexion contracture and the stump must lie alongside the other leg, non-flexed and non-abducted.' Scott rose to his feet. 'I take it the physiotherapist has been alerted?'

Heather knew Peter hadn't had time to do this and was about to jump in with an affirmative to save his face when Peter gave her a gentle smile, which was not missed by the observant Scott. 'No, not yet,' he told the registrar. 'I haven't had time.'

'Do it now,' Scott said without censure. That was reserved for Heather, who was treated to a hard stare. 'I'd like a word with you, Staff, in private,' he said. 'Write up the notes, please, Will.'

'Right, sir.' Will pushed his glasses up his nose, a gesture which showed his nervousness. You could almost see him jumping to attention. He was as tall as Scott, six feet, but slim and not an athlete, preferring more aesthetic pursuits. He was a gentle man whom the patients liked, as did Thomas Blacklock.

Scott will make mincemeat of him, thought Heather, giving Will a sympathetic smile as Scott ushered her out into the corridor. Well, he's not going to chew me up, she thought, though her nerves jangled. What was he going to say?

'I suspect that you were going to lie on the charge nurse's behalf just now,' he said, fixing her with an intent look. 'While I commend loyalty to friends I can't condone lying.'

How had he known? thought Heather, appalled. She felt like a rabbit frozen in the glare of headlights, but she didn't flinch as he continued, 'A patient might suffer, or your gesture might get you into trouble.'

How pompous, Heather thought, while admitting that

the last part of his accusation was valid, though she knew she would never put a patient at risk—ever.

However, she was not going to say, Yes, sir, and creep meekly away. While thinking she would have to be more careful in future when he was around—he was far too intuitive—she spoke up bravely. 'Not in this case. Peter would have contacted the physiotherapist as soon as the round was finished.' Which was true. 'And, in any case—' her anger was rising '—it isn't your place to reprimand the nursing staff—it's Peter's.'

A flash of admiration in his eyes vanished so quickly that Heather didn't see it. 'Perhaps,' Scott conceded. 'But what about answering back to the consultant? Surely that is his prerogative?' Scott raised an eyebrow.

'Not really,' she said, her honesty driving her to add, 'The consultant should report it to the senior nursing officer and she will do the reprimanding.' Heather frowned. 'As, I'm sure, you already know.'

Scott did know, and coudn't understand why he had argued with her. Perhaps it was because she looked so animated when she was angry. The brightness of her seemed to lighten the dim corridor, as he remembered it doing in his hospital room. She was very attractive. 'Do you think I should do that—report you?' he asked, the effect she was having upon him softening his voice.

He was so close she could see the university motif on his tie. She could also smell his aftershave—one she liked. Somehow, here in the corridor, Heather was more than ever aware of him. She held herself stiffly so that he wouldn't suspect just how much.

Her dismay at the feelings he was rousing in her made her answer thoughtlessly, 'It would be one way of getting your own back for the accident.'

'Yes, it would, but I don't happen to be that sort of person,' he told her quietly, her reply effectively dampening his ardour.

Heather felt ashamed. She had instinctively known that. It was just his nearness which had made her blurt out the stupid words.

The uncomfortable silence that stretched between them was broken by the office door opening and Peter saying, 'Excuse me for interrupting.' He gave Heather an anxious look. 'Outpatients are on the line for you, sir.'

'Thanks.' Scott went into the office and closed the door behind him.

CHAPTER FOUR

PETER looked at Heather. 'You OK?' he asked, seeing the troubled look on her face.

'Yes, fine,' she told him with a smile. She could see that Peter wanted to know what had happened between the registrar and herself, but knew that if she told him how Scott had usurped Peter's authority he would be more furious with the new registrar than he was already. 'He was just recalling the last time we met,' she improvised.

'What time's he picking you up, then?' Peter asked with a knowing look.

'Er, he. . .' She was going to add, 'isn't taking me out,' when Scott spoke from behind them.

'Eight o'clock, isn't it, Staff?' Neither of them had heard the office door open as they had been walking towards the ward.

'Er. . .' Heather was so dumbfounded she was speechless.

'You forgot to give me your address,' Scott said blithely.

She told him it in a faint voice, adding, 'It's off Marchmont Road.' There was no way she could avoid agreeing, without telling Peter what she and Scott had been discussing.

'I know where that is,' he said. 'See you, then.'

Scott turned away, astonished with himself for rescuing her by compounding her deceit, for he suspected that she had been going to lie again, though why she should he could not imagine.

He frowned with irritation. This young woman had been the cause of him fracturing his femur, giving him considerable pain and causing him to lose the chance of getting a consultant's post as well. He must be mad. He must have let her remembered kindness at the scene of the accident sway him.

'Would you dress Harry's leg?' Peter asked Heather. The ward work had to continue.

'I'd like to see that pressure sore.' Scott had heard what Peter had said and turned back to join them.

'Come along, then,' Heather said, less than graciously.

Will came out of the office. 'Shall I go ahead to Outpatients?' he asked, having caught the end of the conversation.

'Yes, please,' Scott said. 'I'll join you there.'

Peter went into the office, stiff-backed, and closed the door. 'He'll get used to me,' Scott told Heather as he went into the treatment room.

'We'll all have to do that,' she said tartly.

She was concentrating on pulling out the dressing trolley and didn't see the amusement in his eyes as she laid an unopened dressing pack on the top shelf.

'Why were you going to lie to the charge nurse about our meeting tonight?' Scott asked curiously.

'You shouldn't be so quick to judge people,' Heather said sharply. 'I wasn't going to lie. I was going to deny it. You were the one who lied.' She stood facing up to him like a terrier to an Alsatian.

Scott gaped. 'But you must have said something to give him that impression.'

'He was worried you had told me off,' she said. 'I

couldn't tell him the truth because he's a bit hostile towards you at the moment and it would have increased his dislike so I just told him we were recalling old times and he assumed they were pleasant and that you were taking me out.' Her words tumbled out in a rush.

'I see.' Scott was amused that she had been protecting him.

'So tonight's off,' she said firmly.

'Oh, no,' he assured her. 'Peter is bound to ask how you got on. . .'

'I could make up some excuse,' Heather said, interrupting him.

'No. You'll just have to suffer my company,' he told her. 'You know the old saying—Oh what a tangled web we weave when we practise to deceive.'

There he was, being pompous again, Heather thought. 'All right, but I think you should apply that saying to yourself. I'm not the one who's deceiving him—you are. Can I fetch the patient now?' she asked blithely.

'Yes,' Scott said, rather weakly. He had a funny feeling he had been hoist with his own petard.

Harry Endsworth had fractured his right tibia. It had been a clean fracture and reduced under a general anaesthetic. A full plaster from thigh to toe had been applied.

'Football has a lot to answer for,' Scott said when Heather brought Harry into the treatment room.

Harry was twenty-five, young and active, a sports fanatic. 'I'm missing the rest of the season,' he moaned as he hitched himself onto the examination table with Scott's help.

'You'll be able to watch it, though,' Scott said cheerfully.

'Not the same,' came the disgruntled reply. 'It

wouldn't be so bad if I'd broken my leg in a game, but it happened after I'd been to the match in Glasgow.'

'You fell down the steps of the stadium, I recall,' Scott said.

Heather laid out the dressing pack. 'He had the fracture reduced in Glasgow and insisted on coming home the next day.' She gave Harry a stern look.

'And you didn't contact your GP until the itching drove you mad?' Scott asked.

'My wife did,' Harry told them in an even more aggrieved tone. 'She said she was fed up with my moaning about the burning pain, and she couldn't sleep because I was so restless, and she said my leg smelled.'

'Good job she did,' Scott said. 'But the hospital must have told you to look out for those signs and to contact your doctor if they occurred,' Scott said sternly.

'Yes, but I didn't think it was anything to worry about.'

'His GP was so concerned he had him admitted,' Heather said as she removed the 'window' which had been made in the plaster to treat the pressure sore beneath. She washed her hands, dried them on the towel from the pack and then, using forceps, removed the dressing.

'Doesn't smell now,' Harry said, looking at the almost healed sore with interest.

'That's because it's being treated and you're on anti-biotics,' Scott told him, peering at the wound. 'Is it improving as well as you'd hoped, Staff?' he asked.

Heather was flattered that he should consider her opinion. 'Yes,' she said, smiling at him, 'it's coming along nicely. It only needs a dry dressing now.'

'Good. I'll leave you to finish off, then.'

'Fine.' She was glad when the door closed behind him. Quickly Heather tore open the sachet of saline, poured it onto the swabs and cleaned the area, dried it and applied a dressing. She then put the 'window' back in place, cut strips of micropore to hold it and added a bandage on top as reinforcement.

'Right, Harry,' she said as she helped him off the couch. 'You go and put your leg up.' Her tone was firm. 'I saw you with it down.'

Harry grimaced, but didn't argue.

It was as Heather was clearing up that she realised she hadn't asked Scott how his leg was. I'll ask him tonight, she decided, not without some trepidation, though she hadn't noticed him limping so presumed it must be all right.

'Well, what did the great man think of Harry's wound?' asked Peter sarcastically as she joined him in the office. 'Did it meet with his approval?'

'He was very pleased,' Heather told him.

'I'm relying on you to keep him in a good mood this evening,' Peter said.

'I'll do my best.' She felt aggrieved at having been put into this situation—especially by that man, Scott McPherson.

The rest of the day passed with the usual round of temperatures, dressings, medicines and visits from the physiotherapist.

Heather was off at three, just as the visitors were coming in. She saw how Michael was concentrating on the book he was reading and knew it was to hide his disappointment over not having visitors. She went and chatted with him for a while before she left.

Collecting her bicycle from the porter's lodge, she cycled down the tree-lined bicycle lane which ran from near the hospital through the Meadows. This was a large grassy area which led to Melville Drive.

As Heather rode she marvelled that there could still be such a place free of building in the heart of the city.

Reaching the Drive, she waited for a break in the traffic, then crossed it into Marchmont Road and turned into the street which housed her flat.

Heather found it a much quicker way of travelling to and from the hospital—no waiting for buses and no try-ing to find a parking space, though that didn't apply to her as she didn't own a car.

Gavin wouldn't be home tonight as he was on call and staying at the hospital. She locked up her bicycle and chained it to the banister at the bottom of the stairs.

Letting herself into their flat, she groaned when she found the kitchen looking as if a bomb had hit it. Were all men like this? she wondered as she piled dirty dishes into the washing-up bowl. Was Scott?

When the kitchen was tidy Heather went into the lounge. Gavin's medical journals and climbing maga-zines were scattered on the coffee-table.

Heather's knitting was in a bag by the chair she usually used, and a pair of Gavin's climbing boots which he was checking out for worthiness stood beside his chair.

Heather shuffled the magazines into a pile, plumped up the cushions and flicked a duster over the furniture. The room had a comfortable lived-in look.

She made herself a cup of tea and a sandwich. Lunch had been scrappy and dinner would be late.

What shall I wear this evening? she wondered as she went into her bedroom and threw open the wardrobe door. She ignored the creak of its hinges.

Trousers might be a good idea, she decided as she drew out a black pair, then frowned as she held them up.

These would never fit her now. She'd bought them when she'd lost weight after the break with her fiancé, but she'd gained a few pounds since then.

Should she rush out and buy something? she wondered indecisively as she gazed blankly into the wardrobe. No, I won't, she told herself firmly. I don't know why I'm even thinking of it. I'm not dressing specially for Scott McPherson. He's just an unwelcome reminder of things in the past I want to forget.

I wonder where he'll take me? she mused as she had another rummage amongst her clothes and chose a short black skirt which would look good with the pink jumper her mother had given her last Christmas. Probably the pub, she thought.

Having decided on her clothes, she checked the food cupboard and went out to the local shops nearby to collect some bread.

The rest of the time before Scott was due Heather filled in with her knitting, but as her mind was on what he would say she made so many mistakes that she abandoned it.

Ready, showered and changed well before eight, she fell asleep as she sat in her chair, watching television.

The doorbell rang. Heather leapt to her feet, knocked over her knitting bag and rushed to the door. Still wrapped in sleep, she had forgotten that Scott was expected and thought it was Gavin. He was always leaving his key behind.

She threw the door open and said, 'I'll have to tie it on string round your neck.' Then she saw who it was. 'Oh-h-h!' she said, aghast, and then she laughed. 'I'm sorry. I thought it was my brother, Gavin. He's always leaving his key behind.'

Heather's gleaming red curls were awry, her clothes dishevelled, she was wearing fluffy duck slippers and her eyes were still heavy with sleep. She looked delightfully desirable. Scott had been kicking himself for not taking her up on her offer to cancel the evening, but now he grinned. 'It certainly was an unusual welcome,' he said.

Bother, thought Heather. I'll have to ask him in now. She knew she must look a mess, and hoped she didn't look as flustered as she felt. 'Come into the lounge while I get ready.'

She left him sitting in her chair and went into her bedroom. Quickly she brushed her hair, checked her make-up, then groaned when she realised she still had on her duck slippers.

Perhaps he hadn't seen them, she tried to convince herself as she exchanged them for black court shoes. A short black jacket and shoulder-bag completed her outfit.

Heather had been so flummoxed at Scott's sudden appearance that she couldn't remember what he was wearing. Never mind, she told her reflection in the mirror, adding bravely, I'm dressed for anything.

When she returned to the lounge she found Scott with her knitting in his hand. 'This was on the floor,' he said, his lips twitching as he turned the pterodactyl's wing this way and that, trying to decide what it was.

Oh, bother, she thought. First the duck slippers and now this. 'Thanks,' she said with as much aplomb as she could muster.

'Whoops, careful,' he said, as in her haste to take it from him the stitches came off the needle.

This is definitely not my day, she thought as they both bent ot pick up the pterodactyl's wing and, in doing so, bumped their heads together.

'Do you plan to keep on injuring me whenever we meet?' Scott asked ruefully as he rubbed his head and grimaced.

I'd like to do him a permanent injury to get him out of my hair, she thought. Her face must have shown what she was thinking for he put up his hands. 'Mercy, mercy,' he begged.

Heather had a good sense of humour so she laughed. 'Only if you promise to pick up the stitches.'

'Done.' Carefully he did as he'd been bidden and handed the needle to her.

Surprised, she inspected it minutely. 'I see your surgical skill extends to more than the patients—either that or you learnt to knit at school.'

'I used to pick up stitches for my mother so I've had plenty of practice,' he said laughingly. Then he frowned in puzzlement. 'Just what is that?' He nodded at her knitting.

She drew herself up to her full height. 'A pterodactyl's wing,' she said, daring him to laugh.

'Well, I'm glad it isn't broken as I've no experience in mending pterodactyl's wings.' His face was straight.

There was a moment's pause before she burst out laughing, with him joining in. She wrapped the knitting up and put it carefully into her knitting bag.

The tension his arrival had brought had vanished.

'Shall we go?' Scott gestured for her to precede him. It was then that she noticed he was wearing casual clothes—dark grey trousers and black polo-neck jumper with a black anorak. He looked terrific and her heart hammered in her chest. Her mouth was too dry to reply so she just passed in front of him and locked the door behind them.

As they went down to the street Heather spoke severely to herself. So he's attractive and handsome and the first man to really stir you since Bill, but watch out. You'll just have to keep your hormones in check.

'I've booked a table for us at that new French restaurant in the High Street,' he said, stopping beside a Rover.

'Oh,' she replied, thinking, I hope they don't do nouvelle cuisine. There's never enough on the plate to fill me.

Scott unlocked the passenger door and saw her seated. Thank goodness he didn't bring his motorbike, she thought with relief as she fastened her seat belt.

Scott was lucky in finding a parking space in the road at the back of the castle. As they left the car Heather looked up at the imposing building as it loomed dark above them. She shivered, caught in the grip of history. What ghosts walked there?

'Cold?' Scott asked, linking his arm in hers.

'No,' she said quietly. 'Just wondering what it was like in the old days.'

'Not as good as today,' he said positively, patting her arm comfortingly.

I wish he wouldn't touch me, she thought as his touch roused unwelcome remembered feelings.

'Take medicine, for example. No anaesthetics, no antibiotics.'

He let go of her arm to spread his hands and, contrarily, she missed the warmth of his touch. Poignantly, this brought back that delicious feeling of being loved—the touching, the nuances, the kisses, the fun—and a longing to feel like that again caught hold of her.

'You were lucky to live past forty, and the amount of

food and drink they consumed. . .well,' he had continued while her thoughts roamed.

The mention of food distracted her, and the reminder of how hungry she was helped Heather put those disturbing longings aside. 'Yes, you're right.'

They had reached the Royal Mile. The restaurant was further down, and when they arrived Scott ushered her inside, where his commanding presence brought the head waiter hurrying forward.

As he gave his name Heather looked about her and discovered, to her horror, that it was the sort of place lovers chose—muted lights, tables for two in charming alcoves, soft pink colours and romantic music.

They were shown to their table. As Scott pulled out her seat he said, 'Sorry about this. I had no idea it was this sort of restaurant. One of the doctors recommended it when I asked him to suggest a place to take a young lady.' He took his seat opposite her. 'Probably thought I had romance in mind. Would you rather go somewhere else?'

The humour of the situation struck Heather. Here they were, anything but lovers, dining in this intimate restaurant because of his lie.

However, she suspected that he was feeling a bit uncomfortable, though he didn't show it, so she smiled up at him. 'As long as they have food I don't care where we eat,' she told him. 'I'm ravenous.'

The muted lighting made Heather seem to glow even more. It touched her red hair, putting highlights into it, touched her red lips, which were free of lipstick, and it touched her kind hazel eyes. She was very desirable and his reaction showed in his eyes.

'Well, let's see the menu,' he said, as the waiter handed them one each.

Heather hid her face behind hers. She had seen the way Scott had looked at her and she steeled herself against it.

Heather had no false modesty about her looks. She knew she was attractive, and was grateful for it, but never used it where men were concerned. Now she was even more determined to resist his attractions.

The lighting had been kind to him, smoothing away the lines of experience and seriousness that making life-and-death decisions had etched. It made him look as he must have done ten years ago.

He's more attractive now, she thought, pleased that her newly made decision enabled her to view him dispassionately. He must be about thirty-five, nine years older than herself.

It was the incongruousness of the situation—the pair of them surrounded by lovers—that helped her keep a level head.

Thinking of this reminded Heather of her other decision—to ask how his leg was. The waiter returned just then. Heather ordered French onion soup, hoping it would help to fill her, and pork. Scott chose the soup and chicken.

As soon as the menus had been taken away she said, 'I hate to bring this up, but how is your leg?' Concern, mixed with apprehension, showed clearly in her eyes.

'I wondered when you were going to ask,' Scott said wryly then, seeing the anxiety in her eyes, he added gently, 'It's fine.' A mischievous twinkle entered his eyes. 'I'm not going to ask for you to be removed from the ward.'

Another worry less, thought Heather with relief.

'Thanks for your generosity,' she said in a heartfelt tone.

'Have you been in Edinburgh long?' Scott asked, wanting to know more about this charming, desirable, exasperating woman.

'I trained in London, but was lucky enough to get the staff nurse's post on the orthopaedic ward here,' she explained.

The waiter came with their soup and Scott finished his before he said, 'But you're not a Scot.'

'There you are, presuming again,' she said. 'Just because I have an English accent doesn't mean to say I'm not Scottish.'

The waiter came and removed their empty soup bowls. Scott leaned back in his chair.

'So you are a Scot.' He was pleased he had something firmly established now.

'Well—not exactly,' she said, wishing the main course would appear as only the edge had been taken off her hunger.

'No?' Scott had never met a woman who confused him so.

'No,' Heather said and then, seeing his puzzlement, added, 'I'll explain.'

'Yes, please do,' he implored.

'Well, my father is a farmer—a pig farmer—in the Lake District.' Her eyes became dreamy. It was so romantic how her parents had met. 'He brought his prize pig to Scotland to show at one of the agricultural shows.' She sighed. 'My mother's father was one of the judges and my mother loved to go round all the animals, talking to them to reassure them. She felt sure they would be anxious out of their own environments.' It was obvious to Scott from whom Heather had inherited her warm heart.

'Well, she had climbed onto the top rung of the fencing around my father's prize pig—she's only five feet two,' Heather explained. 'She intended to whisper reassuring words to his pig. My father happened to see her and thought she was about to do his darling pig an injury.' Heather smiled happily. 'He bellowed to her to get off.' Her eyes lost the dreamy look as she focused on Scott.

'He has a loud voice when he wants to use it,' she explained, then paused for a moment to take a sip of the excellent wine he had ordered.

'And?' Scott asked, swept along by her story, and almost wished the warmth in her eyes was for him.

Heather put her glass down. 'Well,' she said confidentially, 'my mother got such a fright she fell into the sty and was covered in muck.' Heather's eyes had become dreamy again. 'Wasn't it romantic?'

'We-e-ll.' Scott tried to keep the laughter out of his voice and the amusement from his eyes because he could see how wonderful she thought her parents' meeting had been, and he didn't want to hurt her. 'It's certainly the most original story I've heard of how two people met.' He didn't add 'apart from us' for he didn't want to cloud the brightness of her eyes.

'Yes,' Heather agreed, then she saw his suppressed amusement and laughed. 'I never thought how funny it was before.'

'So they married and lived happily ever after?' he asked.

'As a matter of fact they did,' she told him simply. 'So, you see now how I am Scottish and yet I'm not.' She looked at him earnestly.

'Yes.' He had a feeling he would never be certain of anything again. 'You're half-Scottish.'

Heather's face brightened. 'That's right.' She sounded as pleased as a teacher would have been with a pupil who had understood her explanation.

The waiter had not appeared with their second course. A frown drew Scott's brows together.

'I expect there's a long time between the courses to allow lovers to talk,' she said, guessing the reason for his frown.

'Well, we're not lovers and we're hungry,' he said, attracting the waiter's attention.

No, nor ever likely to be, thought Heather without even a sigh.

The main course, when it came, was minute in Heather's eyes.

'I take it you're from Edinburgh by your accent?' she asked as she put her knife and fork together, having dispatched her food in record time.

'Yes, I was born in Edinburgh. My parents divorced when I was in my teens,' he said shortly. 'My father was a judge and my mother. . .' His face softened. 'She was a loving person but my father outgrew her, I suppose.' He shrugged. 'Anyway, it doesn't matter now. They're both dead.'

Scott was astonished he'd told her. He'd never thought to tell anyone else. He supposed it was because there was something about this girl that invited confidences, and that you knew she would keep whatever she was told to herself.

Heather heard the sadness in his voice. 'Do you have any brothers and sisters?' she asked gently.

'I only have a younger brother now, who lives with his girlfriend. He's a lawyer.' There was a pause before he added, almost reluctantly, drawn by the compassion he saw in her eyes. 'Another brother between Callum and myself died.'

'Oh, I'm so sorry.' Heather was too sensitive to ask for details. She longed to take the sadness from his eyes, but the grimness of his expression deterred her. His brother must have died in tragic circumstances to put that look on his face.

Taking a deep breath, he asked, 'Would you like a sweet?'

She would have loved a sweet, but knew how expensive these sort of restaurants were so she said, 'No, thanks, just coffee, please.'

Scott had recovered himself by the time they had drunk their coffee. He paid the bill and they left soon afterwards.

'I know how hungry you nurses usually are and I don't want to be responsible for you fading away,' Scott said jokingly, smiling down at her as they walked to collect the car. 'I know a good fish and chip place quite near to where you live.' He settled her into the passenger seat and added, as he took his own beside her, 'How about it?'

'I don't want you to think I'm not grateful for the meal, but that sounds wonderful,' Heather said enthusiastically.

It didn't take them long to reach the fish and chip shop. It was more than a shop—part of it was a café.

There was queue at the counter, but only one other couple was seated at the tables in booths down one side. The seats were vinyl-covered in a tan shade and the tables were plastic-topped for easy cleaning, with sauce bottles grouped together in the centres like soldiers waiting to go into action. The smell of cooking fat hung in the atmosphere.

'Take a seat,' Scott said. 'Fish and chips OK?'

'Yes, please.'

Scott, with his designer clothes and commanding presence, drew instant attention from the man serving, so much so that he tried to take Scott's order ahead of the student in front of him.

'This young man is before me,' Scott said quietly.

Heather liked him for that. He was not an arrogant man, though he did not suffer fools gladly, she suspected.

They were soon eating their fish and chips. 'Mmm,' said Heather appreciatively. 'Lovely.'

'But not too often,' Scott warned as he dipped another chip into tomato sauce. 'Remember how fat can clog your veins and give you a coronary later in life.'

'Is your mind on your profession all the time?' Heather asked drily, his words making her feel guilty as she raised a forkful of fish and chips to her mouth.

'No, not always,' he said softly, looking at her from under lowered lids.

Heather blushed.

Scott laughed. 'Just teasing to make you blush,' he said. 'You don't often see that nowadays.'

Heather took the top off the tomato sauce bottle. 'I think I should make your face red to get my own back,' she threatened, and rose in her seat, her eyes laughing.

'Oh, no.' He put his hands together in a begging pose. 'Please, no. I'll never make you blush again on purpose.'

Heather laughed and sat down. 'You are a comic.'

'My image of the serious professional is ruined,' he said, assuming a doleful expression.

'No,' she said seriously. 'Nothing can take that away from you. It's part of you, like your skin.' Then she smiled and added, to lighten the tone, 'Now eat up your fish supper like a good boy.'

Scott grinned. 'OK.'

They chatted amiably after that.

'Well, you'll be able to give a good report to Peter when you see him tomorrow,' Scott said as they left the chip shop and reached the car.

'Yes, I certainly will,' she agreed, meaning it.

He drove her home. She left the car swiftly. 'No need for you to come up,' she told him, expecting him to nod and drive away—but he didn't.

'Must see you to your door,' he said as he climbed from the driver's seat. 'You never know who might be lurking in the hallway of these flats.'

'Honestly, I do it all the time.'

He frowned. 'Do what all the time?' There she was, confusing him again.

'Come home on my own,' she said, giving him a look that told him she knew exactly what she meant and couldn't understand how he didn't.

'Oh.' He took hold of her arm. 'Nevertheless, I insist.'

Scott went with her to her door, holding her arm all the way. He found he didn't want to let it go. It was a very soft, womanly arm and roused a desire in him to pull her into his own arms, a desire he resisted with difficulty.

'You can unhand me now,' she snapped as they reached the door.

His touch had flustered her so that she fumbled as she searched in her bag for her key.

'Here, let me,' he said, his unsatisfied desire making him exasperated. He grabbed for the shoulder strap.

'No. . .' Too late he had it in his hand.

Scott was astonished as he searched in her bag. No wonder she had difficulty finding her key. First there was a piece of string, which he held up with an enquiring raise of the eyebrows.

'You never know when you might need it,' she explained defensively.

Next came a small box of plasters. He looked at her again. 'The same reason?' he asked.

Heather nodded. Some fruit drops, wrapped in shiny paper, then appeared. He frowned at them. 'They stop children crying on the bus,' Heather told him, not waiting for him to ask.

A small teddy with a sad face came next. 'This?' He raised his eyebrows.

'I just hadn't the heart to leave him at home. He always looks so sad.' She snatched the bear from him and kissed it.

There was an old purse which burst open at his touch, scattering coins all over the floor. 'I should have told you about that,' she said apologetically, as they stooped to pick them up.

She took the now-full purse from him as he delved once more into the bag—to bring out a small packet of tissues, a notebook and pencil. 'To write down things to remind me,' she told him before he asked.

Eventually he found the key. It was attached to a ring from which hung a duck mascot that looked rather worn.

'You must be fond of ducks,' he said, remembering the duck umbrella sheltering him from the rain that fateful day.

He had seen her slippers, Heather thought, mortified, unaware of which duck he was recalling.

'Yes. I sponsor one at the zoo, too,' she told him defiantly.

His lips twitched. 'Very commendable.'

She saw his amusement. He's laughing at me, she thought, and was quite wrong. He found her obsession with ducks and the contents of her bag charming. Not a lipstick or powder compact to be found.

Scott felt his resolve slipping and stiffened it. Thinking of his lost consultancy helped.

Heather snatched the key from his hand and the bag with it. 'Goodnight,' she said, blushing with embarrassment. 'And thank you for a lovely evening.'

She opened the door and slipped quickly inside.

CHAPTER FIVE

'How did the evening go?' Peter asked eagerly next morning when the night staff had gone and Heather was alone with him in the office.

'Fine,' she said truthfully.

'Great.' Peter was pleased. 'Keep up the good work. Must keep the acting consultant happy.' He smiled approvingly at her. 'By the way, would you fetch this X-ray?' He handed her a note of the name. 'Don't want any slip-ups on the round this morning.'

As Heather hurried towards the X-ray department Karen Mackie, the hospital gossip, fell into step beside her. 'Hey, Heather! What's this I hear about you and Scott McPherson?'

'What d'you mean?' Heather asked, horror-stricken. Surely the hospital grapevine wasn't active so soon.

'I saw you both leaving the chip shop,' Karen told her triumphantly. 'You looked very chummy.'

'There's nothing in it,' Heather said sharply.

'Isn't that what people say when they're having an affair and want to keep it dark?' Karen's brown eyes, the colour of her short straight hair, were gleaming.

'Well, it happens to be true this time,' Heather said more forcefully.

'I would have thought he'd have taken you somewhere other than a fish and chip shop,' Karen said disdainfully, ignoring Heather's denial.

'He did. We dined at that new French restaurant.'

59

Heather hastened to defend Scott, though why she should she couldn't imagine. It was his fault she was in this mess.

'That restaurant for lovers?' Karen's eyes became round. 'There must be more between you than you're letting on.'

Heather just managed to hold back a gasp of dismay, but it registered on her face.

'Well, this is where I turn off,' Karen said gaily, stopping at her ward.

'But. . .' Heather was left standing alone for Karen had hurried away, eager to spread the gossip.

Wait till I see that man, Heather thought as she considered strangling Scott.

She hurried back to the ward. 'Where's the X-ray?' Peter asked as she entered the office, still fuming.

'X-ray?' She looked at him blankly.

'Try and keep your mind on your work instead of on Scott McPherson,' Peter said, not unkindly.

If he only knew, thought Heather. 'I'll hurry and get the X-ray now,' she told him, and left quickly.

By the time she returned to the ward the round was about to start. Scott raised an eyebrow at her, skidding to a halt at his feet, as he stood in the office doorway.

'Staff.' He acknowledged her with a nod. He didn't want to smile at her in case she thought he was encouraging her, but she looked so bright-eyed and cheerful that he suddenly did.

That smile sent her heart into a flip. Does he know how devastating his smiles are? wondered Heather, trying to steel herself against him. She then noticed the interest the other nurses and Will were showing in the pair of them. Uh-oh, she groaned to herself. I don't want to be the subject of hospital gossip again.

The round went smoothly—Peter saw to that. Scott stopped at Michael Grant's bed. The young man viewed the new registrar doubtfully. 'I expect you're wondering if I will be as good as Mr Blacklock,' Scott said bluntly, raising an eyebrow. Must be a habit of his, thought Heather.

'Yes,' Michael said, caught off guard.

'Well, all I can tell you is that I know exactly what it's like to fracture your femur. I fractured mine last year, but I was luckier. It was a clean break, whereas your femur was shattered. They managed to pin mine.'

Michael's face brightened. 'How did you have your accident?' he asked with interest.

Scott glanced at Heather, whose face showed her dismay. 'I skidded on a wet road,' he said, with a wry smile in her direction.

'So did I,' Michael said in amazement.

Heather gave Scott a grateful look. No one else seemed to have noticed the interchange.

'We get too many of these motorbike accidents in the ward,' Peter said. 'And some of the injured don't even wear protective clothing.'

'Hmm,' murmured Scott. He had borrowed the motorbike and hadn't been wearing leathers, except for a jacket. He glanced down at the notes. 'How's your back?' he asked, glancing up at Michael.

'Fine now,' Michael said.

'Fine now?' Scott frowned. 'Was it sore?' He glanced enquiringly at Peter.

'Just a bit red yesterday, but it's all right now,' Peter told him stiffly.

'Good.'

Heather saw Peter's back relax and knew he had expected Scott to question him further, something he would have bitterly resented. Peter's nursing care was exceptional and he was very jealous of his reputation.

The round continued. Scott stopped by Ian Ramsay. 'We'll fix you up tomorrow,' he said easily, with the confidence of the skilled surgeon. 'Have you any worries about the operation?'

Ian had always appeared to be a confident, cheerful young man, but now a worried frown altered his face, making it look older. 'Well. . .'

'Yes?' Scott asked encouragingly, looking at Ian kindly.

'Will I be able to play football again?'

'Yes, but try not to damage the other knee,' Scott said, and smiled.

Relief wiped the worry from Ian's face and he grinned. 'I didn't like to ask,' he said, once more his cheerful self.

Heather was impressed. Scott was a commanding figure and in another man this 'presence' might have awed the patients, but the kindness in his eyes and the intuitiveness of his questions reassured them so that they responded to him.

'I'll see you tomorrow,' Scott promised.

'Thanks,' Ian said.

Scott nodded and put his hand out for the next case-note.

Malcolm Simpson was a heavily built man, inclined to obesity. He was in his late forties, brown-haired, with a pleasant round face. 'I see you have successfully reduced your weight, Mr Simpson,' Scott said with approval, 'so now we'll be able to operate tomorrow and relieve your bunions.'

'Thanks, Doctor.' Scott was about to move on when he saw a puzzled frown on Malcolm's face. 'Something worrying you?' Scot asked, turning back.

'Not worrying, exactly, just curious,' Malcolm said.

Scott looked at him enquiringly with his head on one side. 'Yes?'

'Well, why did I have to lose weight?' Malcolm asked mildly. 'I could understand it if I was having a stomach operation—but my feet?'

'It's the anaesthetic,' Scott explained. 'Post-operatively it's better for you if you're not overweight. You're less likely to contract chest infections. Also, you won't be carrying so much weight when you start walking again.' He smiled. 'OK?'

'Thanks.' Malcolm nodded.

The last patient was George Wilson, who had been admitted after Scott had finished the round yesterday. He was man of sixty, of medium build, with thinning brown-grey hair and blue eyes.

Scott smiled reassuringly. He had noted how depressed the patient looked and also observed the lines of pain imprinted on George's face. 'You'll be pain-free once you've had your hip replaced,' Scott said with assurance.

'I'll believe that when it happens,' George said dispiritedly. 'I've heard the operation isn't always successful.'

'It will be in your case,' Scott said firmly.

George's face brightened a bit at the assurance in Scott's tone, but he was still doubtful. 'Well. . .'

'I can promise you that you'll be fine, and I don't make promises lightly.' His expression was serious. 'I've had some experience of pain myself, but cannot begin to know how much you have suffered,' he said sincerely, looking at George compassionately. 'We can't allow that to continue and I mean to correct it tomorrow.'

George was impressed. 'You really understand.' He seemed astonished.

'I'm glad you think so,' Scott told him. 'I'll see you in Theatre tomorrow.'

Scott turned away and glanced round the ward. 'Why isn't Alan McDermott in the ward?' he asked.

Heather knew that Peter had deliberately left Alan in the side-ward. 'I didn't think you meant him to be transferred until today,' the charge nurse said, his head raised defiantly.

'Oh,' Scott said mildly. 'We'd better go and see him there, then.'

Heather didn't realise that she had been holding her breath until she had to let it go. It came out in a loud sigh.

Scott cast a look in her direction and raised one eyebrow.

Alan was looking much better when they entered his room. 'We're keeping him pain-free,' Peter said evenly. 'His bandage had been reapplied regularly and there's no sign of haemorrhage.'

Scott had a look at the charts. 'Everything is going along nicely,' he told Alan. 'Charge Nurse will have you moved into the ward today.' He gave Alan a searching look. 'OK?'

Alan took a deep breath. 'Yes. The sooner I meet people the better,' he said bravely.

Scott patted him on the shoulder. 'Good man,' he said with approval.

They left him and went into the office.

Heather waited for Scott to explode. She could see

that Will was also, so she was pleasantly surprised when Scott said, 'You were quite right not to move Alan for forty-eight hours, Peter.' He smiled at the charge nurse. 'I should have mentioned that. Thank you.'

Peter's stiff face relaxed. 'Coffee?' he asked.

'Yes, please,' Scott replied.

The tense atmosphere of yesterday had gone. Scott was a fair man. He was ready to admit he had overlooked something, just as he was ready to reprimand if it was needed.

The coffee came, the notes were written up and Scott rose to leave.

'Could I have a word with you, please, Mr McPherson?' Heather asked, aware that her words had riveted the staff's attention but that couldn't be helped. She had to talk to Scott.

Scott glanced at his watch. 'I can give you two minutes, Staff,' he said easily. 'Walk with me to the end of the corridor.' He glanced at Will. 'You go ahead to Female Orthopaedics.'

Outside the office the only sound at that moment was that of Will's scurrying feet. 'Well, Heather?' Scott asked encouragingly.

His nearness was disconcerting her and she blurted out, 'Do you realise what your lie to Peter has resulted in?'

The smile left Scott's face. 'I wasn't aware that I had lied,' he said tersely.

'I didn't mean it that way,' she hastened to say. 'I—'

'What way did you mean?' he asked, frowning in exasperation.

'We were seen by one of the hospital gossips, coming out of the chip shop, and the whole hospital thinks we're dating,' she told him in a rush.

'I noticed I was being viewed with more than the usual curiosity,' Scott said, his frown deepening.

'Yes, well. . .' Heather stumbled for a moment, surprised at the consideration he seemed to be giving the matter. She had prepared herself for him to treat it lightly.

'It would be no good our avoiding each other either,' he said seriously. 'Everyone would only be more convinced.'

'Er, yes,' she agreed in pleased astonishment.

'I haven't time to discuss it now,' he said briskly. 'When are you off?'

'Three o'clock,' she told him.

'Hmm.' He thought for a moment. 'I'm busy all afternoon so that's out.' His brows drew together in a frown. 'It'll have to be this evening. I'll pick you up at six.'

He was gone before she could tell him she was going out. It was her night for visiting Len and she couldn't put that off. She watched his figure striding impatiently away. I'll just have to try and catch him at his office, she thought.

Heather was kept busy until it was time for her to go off duty. The visitors were coming in and she was just about to leave the ward when Mike called her over. 'Could you get me a special birthday card for my mum?' he asked, leaning over to reach in his locker for his money.

'Sure,' Heather said with a smile. 'Do you want it with "Mother" on it?'

'Yes, please, and could you send some flowers for me?'

'Of course.' She accepted the money he was handing over. 'When is her birthday?'

'Day after tomorrow,' he said a bit wistfully.

'I'm sure they'll be able to come down soon,' she said sympathetically, hoping she was right.

'Yes,' he said, but dolefully.

'Look, I'll stay and chat for a while,' she said, thinking she would still be able to catch Scott a bit later.

Mike's face brightened. 'Thanks,' he said gratefully. 'I'm OK in the mornings,' he confided. 'The other patients stop for a chat. It's just visiting time I feel it.'

Heather drew a chair close to the bed. 'I can understand that,' she said compassionately.

She stayed until four o'clock when visiting was over.

'Thanks, Staff,' Mike said gratefully.

Heather smiled as she replaced the chair against the wall. 'See you tomorrow.'

She glanced at her watch as she hurried along the corridor to Scott's office. It was four-fifteen—surely he would still be there.

His secretary was just coming out when Heather arrived. 'What a pity, you've just missed him,' she said, smiling at Heather. She gave a small, dreamy sigh. Roberta Smith was fifty—and another romantic. 'He's such a nice man,' she said. 'If I were twenty years younger and not happily married I might give you a run for your money.'

Heather groaned inwardly. If the secretaries knew then word had spread more quickly than she had thought.

Well, no use denying it. She would just have to wait and see what Scott would suggest, but when he came she would tell him that she couldn't see him tonight.

Heather hurried to buy the card for Mike and order the flowers. As she dressed in black jeans and green jumper she was glad her brother wasn't at home.

She was ready when the doorbell rang at six o'clock and she opened the door to Scott.

CHAPTER SIX

'YOU left me so quickly I couldn't tell you I can't see you tonight. I'm seeing Len,' Heather said with a worried frown. 'I tried to catch you at your office, but you'd gone.'

'Len your boyfriend?' Scott asked, feeling a touch of envy which he quickly suppressed.

'No, of course not.' Heather shook her head.

'Well, can't you put him off?'

'Oh, no,' she told him seriously. 'Len's a super bloke. We had him in briefly as a patient before he was transferred to the spinal unit in Glasgow.' They were in the hall and the light showed the compassion in her eyes, which was reflected in her voice. 'He's twenty-five and a paraplegic.'

'Is it wise to become involved with your patients outside work?' he asked gently.

'I don't normally,' she said. 'But Len's wife is my friend, Janet, and she did. She was on Orthopaedics when Len came in and she fell in love with him.' She glanced at Scott. 'Wasn't that romantic?'

'Nurses and patients often fall in love, as do doctors and nurses,' Scott said dismissively.

'Have you ever fallen in love with a nurse?' Heather asked curiously.

'No, and I don't intend to,' he confessed. 'I plan to keep my professional life and private life separate.'

Good, thought Heather. Anyway, he's the sort who

69

has glamorous women on his arm, not someone who wears duck slippers. She smiled at the thought.

I wonder what she's smiling at? wondered Scott curiously. 'If I come with you,' he said, 'we can have our talk afterwards.'

'OK.'

She locked the flat and preceded him out to the car. As they took their seats Scott said, 'You'll need to direct me.'

'They live in a bungalow off Queensferry Road,' she told him.

'Oh, I know where that is.' Scott put the car into gear and drove away.

It had started to rain. The wipers swished back and forth across the windscreen. 'I like the rain,' Heather said, looking out at the watery streetlights. 'There's something fresh and cosy about it. I always think of warm fires, crumpets for tea and a good book.' She hugged her voluminous bag to her.

'Hmm. Romance plays a big part in your life, doesn't it?' Scott said as he carefully manoeuvred the car down the street, narrowed because of parked cars.

'Yes, I suppose it does,' Heather agreed. 'There's nothing wrong in that, is there?' she asked defensively, thinking she had heard a note of censure in his voice.

'Not as long as you keep it in perspective,' he said evenly. 'You can't live your life looking through rose-coloured spectacles all the time.' He sounded impatient.

'As a nurse, I see enough of the sad side of life to know that,' she said sharply, resenting his tone. 'But it doesn't do any harm to dream.'

'No, I suppose not,' he agreed. 'I expect I'm that much older than you and have become cynical.'

'Oh, no.' She hastened, as usual, to reassure. 'You're just a realist. You think with your head instead of your heart.'

She was very perceptive, this young woman, thought Scott. 'It comes with age,' he told her.

'Oh, I hope it doesn't happen to me,' she said earnestly.

He cast a sideways look at her. Even in the darkened car she seemed to glow. Seeing her troubled eyes, he said gently, 'I'm sure it won't.' He realised he was doing the same thing as she did—rushing to reassure without thinking—but it was worth it to see her face shine cheerfully again.

Scott drove through the city. He had to stop at the traffic lights at the junction of Lothian Road and Princes Street. 'It's great to be back in Edinburgh,' he said, looking up Princes Street to the right. 'It's a beautiful city even in the rain.'

Heather could hear the pride in his voice. 'Yes. I love this city, too.' She followed his glance up the street. 'You don't feel the buildings are towering above you like you do in some cities. The castle and gardens on the right with the shops on the left, lining just one side of the street, make it look spacious.'

'I like the sense of history here.'

'I do, too,' Heather said happily.

The lights changed and Scott took a left turn, away from the city centre.

'Was the accident the cause of Len's injury?' he asked.

'Yes,' Heather said. 'It was during the winter and the roads were icy. Len was coming back to Edinburgh from a gymnastic event—he was being considered for the Olympics—when the car was involved in a pile-up.' Her tone was sad. 'Len's father was driving and was killed.

Len was in the passenger seat and a well-meaning person dragged him from the car—no neck support, no back support.' Heather sighed.

'He was paralysed from the waist down. Tragic because if he had had professional attention he would not have been paralysed.

'How sad,' Scott said compassionately. 'You would think everyone would know not to move a person at an accident by now, except to lift the head off the chest to prevent suffocation by the tongue. Unless there was a danger of fire?'

'Yes,' Heather agreed. 'Turn left here,' she instructed him. 'It's the last bungalow on the right.'

Scott drew up outside a bungalow identical to the rest in the road. It was sturdily built and not modern.

Heather pulled the black umbrella with the duck handle from her bag and waited for Scott to join her. He took the umbrella from her with a smile. 'Just the sort of weather for ducks,' he teased, as he held the umbrella over them both with one hand and put his other arm about her to draw her closer out of the rain.

Heather had to quell an overwhelming desire to snuggle against him as she laughed. She felt, instinctively, that he was the sort of man who would protect the one he loved—who would put his arm about her just to feel close to her. But she must quell these thoughts for Bill had been a toucher.

Scott closed the umbrella. 'Madam,' he said as he gave it to her with a small bow, 'allow me to present your duck.'

'You are a fool,' she said, forgetting for a moment that he was her acting consultant as she rang the bell.

'Well, don't let the hospital grapevine hear you say

that or I'll be out of a job.' His face was serious.

Before Heather could wonder why, Janet Kinnaird had opened the door. 'Heather,' she said with pleasure. 'I thought you might not be coming.'

'Sorry to be late,' Heather apologised. 'Blame it on Scott. I hope you don't mind me bringing him along.'

'No.' Janet gave Scott a friendly smile as she opened the door wider. 'Len will be delighted. He loves meeting new people.'

The wide hall was decorated in pale beige with a dark carpet which hid the wheelchair's runner marks.

Janet led them into a large lounge. It was light and airy with pastel-coloured decor. There were four armchairs, covered in the same material as the curtains. A three-piece suite would have taken up room needed for the wheelchair. A coffee-table with magazines scattered over its top and a large bookcase completed the furniture.

Len swung his wheelchair to face them. 'Hi, Heather. Who's your friend?'

'Scott McPherson,' Scott said, holding out his hand and smiling easily.

'I diagnose a doctor in the house,' Len said, giving Scott a firm handshake.

'How did you guess?' Scott asked in astonishment.

'There was no hesitation in your glance,' Len explained. 'No embarrassment.' There was a look of acceptance in his eyes as he added, 'Like there is with some people who have no experience of folk in my position.'

'Yes,' Janet said calmly. 'People are inclined to ignore someone in a wheelchair, not even bothering to talk to them but talking to whoever is with them instead.' Her tone was grim. 'They'll say things like, "How is he today?" as if Len were a baby.'

Len laughed. 'When that happens Janet looks down at me and says, "Well, baby, how are you today? Goo, goo, goo, goo". It either sends the speaker scurrying away or they get the message and apologise.'

'Good for you,' Scott said, looking at Janet with admiration.

Janet put her arm round Heather's shoulders. 'But people like Heather make up for all the humiliation,' she said with a smile. 'She'll do anything she can to raise funds for us.'

'Oh,' Scott said quietly.

'Well, I'm glad she's roped you in to help,' Len said. 'I—'

'Scott's not here for that reason,' Heather hastened to explain. 'He's much too busy with his work as a consultant orthopaedic man.'

'Acting consultant,' Scott said swiftly, with a small frown. He had too much integrity to like being misrepresented. 'And I'm never too busy to help a good cause.'

Heather had noted the frown and misread the reason for it. She thought it was because she had reminded him of his lost opportunity, and she groaned inwardly.

A change of subject was indicated, and quickly, she decided. Heather set her large bag on the couch and drew out a succession of soft knitted toys. There were teddy bears in different sizes and colours, some with slightly uneven legs and arms, pandas, dogs and even dolls.

'I'm still knitting the prehistoric animals, but I should have them ready for your stall at your church's Christmas fair,' she told Len.

'Thanks,' Len said. 'Are you sure we can't give you some money for the wool?'

'No,' Heather assured him. 'I pick up odd balls in the sales. It costs very little.'

'Well, thanks very much.'

Janet had left the room, but returned shortly. Pretty china cups rattled in their saucers as she pushed a trolley. A teapot with a knitted cover, which Scott wondered if Heather had knitted, a sugar bowl and milk jug were also on the top shelf. A large chocolate cake was on the bottom with plates, cake forks and napkins.

'The kettle's ready to make coffee, if you'd prefer it,' Janet told Scott.

'No, tea will be fine,' he assured her.

They took off their anoraks and Janet whisked them away. The tea was poured, the cake cut and each had a piece. 'Mmm,' Heather said as she finished her first mouthful. 'This cake's the best you've ever made.'

'Heather always says that.' Janet gave her friend an indulgent smile.

'It's certainly the best cake *I've* ever eaten,' Scott said, endorsing Heather's praise.

'You can come again, Scott,' Janet joked.

'I wish I could make them like this,' Heather said wistfully. 'Mine always sink in the middle.'

'You just need practice,' Janet assured her. 'I make cakes all the time,' she told Scott. 'That's what I do, and it's something I can do at home.'

'She's very successful at it as well,' Len said proudly.

'Thanks, husband, dear,' Janet said, giving him a smile. 'But cake-making can't compare with how you create computer programmes.'

'Computers I find difficult, Len,' Scott admitted.

'Perhaps you could give me a few pointers.'

'With pleasure.' Len's blue eyes brightened. 'As soon as you've finished your tea, if you like.'

'Perhaps Scott and Heather have other plans,' Janet suggested.

'I haven't—have you, Heather?' Scott gave her an enquiring look.

The only plan Heather had was to have a chat with Scott so all she could say was, 'No.'

She helped Janet wash the dishes while Scott went with Len to the room that had been converted into an office.

'Scott's nice,' Janet said, too innocently. 'How long have you known him?'

'Two days,' Heather said, drying a plate.

'Two days?' Janet nearly dropped the cup she was washing. 'I thought you'd known each other for ages.'

It seems like that to me, too, thought Heather wryly. He's been on my mind since the accident. 'Have you many orders for cakes?' she asked, to distract her friend.

'Yes,' Janet said, accepting the change of subject. 'Word of mouth has spread and I've just about as much as I can handle.' She took off her washing-up gloves and put them away.

They went back into the lounge and chatted about friends they both knew until Scott and Len joined them. Heather rose. 'I think we'd better be going,' she said.

'Well, I hope you'll let me come again,' Scott asked. 'I'll need a lot more lessons.'

'Just give me a phone call when you're free,' Len told him.

They both came to the door to see their guests out.

'Lovely couple,' Scott said as they took their seats in

the car. 'You don't think of him as being in a wheelchair, do you?'

'You don't and I don't, but others don't see the man— they just see the wheelchair,' Heather said, compassion for her friends lighting her eyes.

Scott nodded. 'I'll run you home.'

'I thought we were going to have a chat,' Heather said sharply.

'Of course. I'd almost forgotten,' Scott said. 'Do you want to go to your place or mine?'

'My brother will be home so we'd better go to your place.'

The rain had stopped, but the street lighting made the roads glisten.

Scott turned into the underground garage of his block of flats. 'Nice and near the hospital,' Heather said as she stepped out.

He took her arm and she didn't pull away. 'These flats were converted from an old house,' he told her.

The lift zoomed silently up to the second floor. Her feet made no sound on the carpeting as she walked beside him to number seven. 'My lucky number, that,' she said.

'You're superstitious as well as romantic?' he asked.

'Isn't everybody?' she asked as he turned the key in the lock.

'D'you mean romantic or superstitious?' He ushered her in.

'I'm sure you do that deliberately,' she said, her annoyance with him preventing her from seeing the off-white decor of the hall or the dark grey carpet.

'Do what deliberately?' he asked, exasperation sounding in his voice as he ushered her into the lounge.

'Misunderstand me,' she told him indignantly.

'Well you do have rather a feather-brain at times,' he said, his eyes amused as he looked at the bright-eyed, red-haired, vibrant young woman standing so indignantly before him.

'I don't know how you can say that,' she said, stung by his accusation. 'I know exactly what I mean.'

'Good.' Scott felt he was sinking deeper into a morass. 'It's obviously me that's at fault. I'll try harder next time to understand you,' he said wryly.

'Oh, it's not your fault,' Heather hurried to reassure him, unaware of the sarcasm in his voice. 'My brother complains as well,' she confessed. 'Women understand me. You can't help being a man.'

'No, I suppose not,' he said drily. 'Can I take your jacket?'

Warnings from her mother never to be alone with a man in his flat flashed through Heather's mind. Do grow up, she thought. This man certainly has no designs on your body.

She took it off and handed it to him. 'Coffee?' he asked.

'Yes, please.'

While he was away she looked about her. The walls were decorated with an ivory-coloured paper, its delicate design almost invisible, and the mantelpiece was white. The carpet was grey and the three-piece suite black leather. There were stark grey and black-and-white pictures of cubes and angles on the wall and cubic ornaments. It seemed so out of character. Maybe this flat showed another side of Scott, Heather mused.

She shivered just as Scott returned with two mugs on a tray and a plate of biscuits. 'Are you cold or is it the decor?' he asked as he put the black wooden tray onto the black coffee-table.

'The decor,' she said honestly.

'Yes, it is a bit grim, but not of my choosing,' he explained, glancing at it. 'I'm just renting the flat until I get a place of my own.'

'I wonder if the person who owns the flat suffers from depression,' Heather mused, her tone sympathetic as she accepted the mug from him and added a spoon of sugar.

'Could be,' Scott agreed, glancing at the pictures. 'Have a biscuit?' He offered her the plate of rich tea biscuits. 'I'm afraid they're not very exciting.'

'I like these,' Heather assured him, taking one and nibbling it.

'Do you always try to make life easier for people?' Scott asked softly.

'No,' Heather replied swiftly. Although his tone was gentle, Heather felt he was implying that she was lying when she said she liked the biscuits. 'I do like these biscuits.' She finished the one she was eating and took another.

'I wasn't criticising,' Scott said, with a laugh.

Heather grinned. 'Sorry. I thought you were.'

Scott finished his biscuit and took a sip of his coffee. 'Look, about this rumour—'

'Yes,' she interrupted him. 'What can we do to squash it?'

'Well, I could treat you coldly,' Scott suggested.

'That might work, but—'

'Hmm.' It was his turn to interrupt her. 'Maybe it would be better if we go on seeing each other for a while, then tail off. It would seem more natural that way.'

Heather wondered if that would be a good idea. She

liked being with him—more than liked, if she was
honest—and if she saw more of him it might end in
heartache for her. She must think with her head and
not her heart this time, she told herself.

Heather did this, but couldn't think of anything better
than his plan. 'OK,' she agreed.

'I think we should have a few ground rules.' His tone
was serious. 'There's no denying we're attracted to each
other, but I want to make it plain that I never get romantically involved with the nursing staff. It causes too many
problems at work.'

Conceited man, Heather thought, containing her anger
with difficulty. 'Have no fear where I'm concerned,' she
said with dignity. 'I have no intention of becoming, as
you say, romantically involved with anyone for a long,
long time—especially with a doctor.' She added, to
reinforce her declaration, 'They make lousy husbands.'

Scott wanted to laugh, and managed to control himself
only with difficulty. 'Well, now that we've settled that
I'll take you home.'

Heather was still on her dignity. 'I can walk.'

Scott shook his head. 'I'll take you home,' he said
firmly.

It took only minutes to reach her street, though he had
to park a little distance away. 'When are you off this
week?' he asked easily as he walked beside her.

'At three o'clock all this week,' she told him snappily,
wishing she'd never suggested they do something about
the hospital grapevine.

'I have engagements for the next two evenings, but
what about Friday?'

'That would be fine,' she told him briskly.

'Good.'

Scott insisted on seeing her to her flat, but this time her key was in her pocket so she didn't have to search for it.

Heather opened the door and turned to face him. Taking her by the shoulders, he couldn't resist drawing her close to kiss her lightly on the lips.

'That's not part of the bargain,' she told him, using anger to hide how much the light touch of his lips had affected her.

'It was just a brotherly kiss.' he said cheekily.

'I've got a brother. I don't need another one,' she told him sharply. 'What I need is a friend.'

She looked so troubled that he wished he hadn't given way to the sudden desire which had made him kiss her.

'I *am* your friend, Heather,' he said gently, giving her a hug.

'In that case. . .' she stood on tiptoe and kissed his cheek '. . .thanks, and goodnight.'

With a wave of his hand he was gone.

CHAPTER SEVEN

HEATHER and Scott settled into a routine. On the ward he treated her with the professionalism he used with all the staff, but socially their relationship was friendly. It was their awareness of each other that made it far from easy.

Two weeks later Ian Ramsay, his knee needing only physiotherapy, Harry Endsworth, his wound now healed, and Malcolm Simpson had been discharged. Alan McDermott had been transferred to a hospital in Glasgow nearer his family.

On Monday Heather returned from lunch to find Peter sorting out the patients' notes. 'Thanks for keeping our acting consultant happy, Heather,' he said, glancing up. 'The ward is benefiting by it.'

'I can't take credit for that,' she said quickly. 'Scott's just a good doctor and cares for the patients.'

'Jumping to defend him?' Peter smiled at her. 'You two—'

'Isn't it great how well Mr Wilson has progressed after his hip replacement?' Heather interrupted quickly, to distract Peter.

'Yes.' Satisfaction showed in Peter's eyes. 'It was freedom from pain that did it.'

'And Scott's positive approach,' Heather said, without thinking.

Peter laughed. 'There you go again.'

'I'm only speaking the truth. I'd do the same for anybody,' she said defensively.

Peter's face became serious. 'OK. OK. You're quite right.' He put the case notes in a tidy pile. 'He's an excellent doctor.' Then he added, with a frown, 'I might not approve of all his ideas—and he is inclined to usurp my job at times—but I can't fault his kindness to the patients.'

'You're thinking of George Wilson,' Heather said, then wished she'd never mentioned the name. It was a sore point with the charge nurse.

'Yes.' Peter frowned.

'But surely contacting Mr Wilson's daughter was an act of kindness,' Heather rushed in.

'Yes, but that was my job, really.' Peter's frown deepened.

'I think it was just that Mr Wilson found Scott approachable,' she said.

'And the patients don't find me so—is that what you mean?' Peter thumped the case-notes down on the desk.

I do get myself into hot water, thought Heather, wondering how she was going to smooth this over. 'Of course not,' she said swiftly, thinking rapidly. 'You weren't on duty when he spoke to Scott.'

That wasn't strictly true. Peter had been on his lunch break when Scott had appeared in the office. 'I've just seen George Wilson,' he'd told Heather, popping into the office.

'Peter's at lunch,' she'd told him. 'Anything wrong?'

'Not really. I sensed something was worrying George when I did the ward round yesterday. I had a minute to spare so I thought I'd pop in and see him.'

'Oh—and?'

'Apparently, he fell out with his daughter and now that he's pain-free he wants to make it up with her.'

'Can you tell me the reason for the break-up?' Heather asked.

'Yes,' he said. 'His pain was increasing and he was finding it difficult to get around.' He leant against the office wall and folded his arms. The light from the window shone on his face. No wonder he looked tired, doing two jobs, she thought, and her heart went out to him.

'He has only one daughter and she's married with four young children. He didn't want to burden her further so he picked a fight with her on purpose to drive her away.'

'That was thoughtful of him,' Heather said, remembering how Trevor Cameron had had to be reminded about his daughter who had been in a similar situation.

'Perhaps you're right.' He unfolded his arms and came closer to her, feeling a need to absorb the warmth that seemed to emanate from her. 'Anyway, I have to go.'

If there hadn't been this intense attraction between them Heather would have given him a hug, but she felt it might break the fine line that held them apart so she resisted with difficulty.

She uncapped her ballpoint. 'If you give me the name, address and phone number I'll contact Mr Wilson's daughter and explain.'

'No, I said I would see to it,' Scott said shortly. Her nearness was disturbing him more than he wanted. He had his hand on the doorknob when he turned back. 'You'd better mention it to Peter, though.'

He had gone before she could reply. What a kind man he was, she thought. Nothing was too much trouble for him where the patients were concerned.

Heather decided not to tell Peter because she knew he'd be hurt that Mr Wilson hadn't spoken to him and so would be hostile towards Scott.

It all came out anyway when George Wilson's daughter came to see him and asked Peter to thank Scott for contacting her. Heather had been off duty at the time.

It was the next day that Peter had confronted Scott, who had looked at Heather in puzzlement. 'I thought you were going to tell Peter.'

'I—'

'Forgot to,' Scott had said angrily. He had a busy outpatients session that afternoon, added to which he had to suppress the desire which rose to plague him every time he saw her.

'Not exactly. . .' Heather was angry as well.

'Let it be,' Peter had said. 'The patient's happy and that's all that counts.'

His words had silenced them but Heather was not going to let Scott think she was inefficient, and later that day she caught him at the end of his outpatients session.

Scott had been sitting behind his desk and looked up as she came in. 'Sorry I snapped,' he said, before she could speak. He rubbed his hands over his face.

Immediately she wanted to reassure him. 'That's OK,' she said gently, her anger dissipating. 'I thought you looked tired and wondered if you would like to call off our date tonight?' She lied, compassion for him wiping away the real reason for her visit.

He rose from the desk and put his arm round her shoulders. 'Would you mind?'

'Of course not. An early night would do us both good.' She reached up and kissed his cheek, wanting more— wanting much more—but suppressing the urge. 'See you tomorrow,' she said quickly, and rushed away from the desire she had seen flare in his eyes.

'Sorry for that flash of temper,' Peter said. 'I'm going to lunch.'

Heather pushed her thoughts aside. 'Right.'

She took the drug-cupboard keys from Peter and left the office with him to go into the ward. 'Hey, Staff,' Michael called, waving a letter. 'My parents are coming at the weekend.' The boredom had left his face. 'Isn't that great?'

'It certainly is,' she agreed, smiling happily for him.

'Did you hear Mr McPherson say I might be off this frame by Christmas?'

'Indeed I did,' she confirmed. 'But he also said it would be up to Mr Blacklock.'

Disappointment flashed in Michael's eyes for a moment, then it was swept away. 'I have great faith in Mr McPherson. If he says I'll be up by Christmas then I will be.'

'That's the way to think,' she told him.

As she turned away George Wilson touched her arm. 'I want to thank you and all the nurses for your kindness,' he said, pushing a box of chocolates into her hand. 'And would you give this to Mr McPherson?' He handed her a bottle of whisky. 'It was so good of him to go and see my daughter.'

Heather assumed Scott had phoned Mr Wilson's daughter and was impressed. 'I'll see he gets it,' she said. 'And thanks for the chocolates. We'll all enjoy them.'

Heather went back to the office, glad that Peter was on his lunch-break. She groaned. Peter would be hurt again, not because he would envy the gift for Scott but because he was still smarting over the reason for it. She would have to hide the whisky from him.

Heather was just looking round the office for a place when the door opened. She swung round, her heart thumping—thinking Peter had returned early—but it was Scott and her heart thumped even more.

'Drinking on duty?' he asked with a raised eyebrow.

'Thank goodness you're here,' she said, worry that it might be Peter still in her eyes.

'What's happened?' he asked quickly, her anxiety disturbing him. 'Is Colin Watson OK?' His brows drew together in a frown. 'I know the X-ray showed just a crack in his pelvic ring but there's always a risk the X-ray didn't reveal everything.'

'He's passing urine OK and there's no blood in it,' she told him, understanding his worry. 'And all his vital signs are fine.'

Colin Watson had been admitted forty-eight hours ago. He had sustained a fractured pelvis and two cracked ribs in a car accident.

'Good, but was there something else?' He raised his eyebrows enquiringly.

'Nothing to do with work. It's just that Mr Wilson wants you to have this.' She held up the bottle of whisky.

Scott's eyes gleamed. 'Mmm!' He reached for it, but Heather held it away from him.

Scott grinned. 'Game time, is it?' He made a lunge for the bottle.

'Scott. . .' She tried to dodge him, but was caught in his arms.

His nearness set her already-raised pulse scampering even faster. She was so close to him that she could feel his heartbeat quicken.

Heather looked up into his face and saw the desire that had quickened her body reflected in his eyes before his lips came down upon hers in a kiss that shook them both.

Angrily, she pushed him away. 'You're breaking our bargain,' she snapped at him, controlling her trembling body with difficulty.

Bill's kiss had never affected her like this and she was furious—with herself for responding, and with Scott because she knew it could go no further.

'Sorry,' he murmured.

Collecting herself, she handed him the whisky. 'I was going to hide it until I could give it to you without Peter knowing,' she told him. 'But you can have it now.'

Scott was angry with himself and with her and fought to control it. Damn Mr Wilson and damn Heather Langley. 'Why?' he said, his voice still rough with desire.

'Because he was hurt Mr Wilson hadn't asked him to contact his daughter, and this thank-you gift to you would just compound it.'

He slammed the whisky down on the desk. 'Give it to Peter. Tell him Mr Wilson wanted him to have it for the hospital Christmas party,' he said in an uptight voice.

'Peter will just thank him, though, and Mr Wilson will tell him—'

Scott felt like screaming. This woman was the most aggravating female he had ever met. He interrupted her. 'Give it to him when Mr Wilson has gone,' he said through gritted teeth, glaring at her.

'Good idea,' Heather said briskly. 'But you don't have to glare at me.'

'I could shake you, Heather Langley,' Scott said tersely.

'Because your mind doesn't work like mine, or because I attract you?' she asked bluntly.

'Both.'

'It's not my fault I'm a *femme fatale*,' she said innocently.

There was silence between them for a moment, then Scott laughed uproariously. 'Heather Langley, you really are terrific, and if I were a marrying man I'd have you at the top of the list.'

Huh! Heather thought. Conceited man. 'Thanks a bunch,' she said wryly, 'but I couldn't possibly be responsible for you breaking your rule about not having nurses in the family.'

Scott laughed again.

Heather picked up the whisky and hid it at the back of the stationery cupboard.

'Did you come for anything special?' she asked, thinking it was time they found firmer ground.

'No. I just popped in to see how Colin is,' Scott told her.

'Doctor's intuition working?' Heather asked.

'Not really.' He didn't sound too sure about that. 'Just worried about him. I felt he should have been sent to the intensive care unit for forty-eight hours, with all those grazes and bruising, in case we missed anything but they were full.' He frowned. 'So many accidents these days.' He sighed. 'I don't want him suffering from secondary shock.'

'Well, he seems to be coping all right,' Heather said gently. She was disturbed because she had never seen Scott show his anxiety like this before. He always seemed so confident and assured.

'We're keeping a close eye on him and David's with

him,' she told him reassuringly. 'You said yourself there was no bruising in the bladder area.'

'Yes, I know, and I have complete confidence in the staff.' He rubbed a hand over his forehead. 'I'm just a bit tired, and when you're tired things get blown out of proportion.' He smiled ruefully. 'Sorry.'

'Were you called in to help at that pile-up just outside Glasgow?' Heather asked intuitively.

'Yes. The casualties were taken to Glasgow, but they needed another orthopaedic surgeon to help.' He shook his head. 'What a shambles it was. Injured people everywhere. I had to amputate on an unconscious patient on the spot again.' His shoulders sagged a little. 'I don't like doing that. The patient suffers such trauma afterwards when they regain consciousness and find a limb missing.'

She pulled out the desk chair and pushed him into it. 'You saved a life. That's what you have to think about,' she told him firmly.

He looked up at her with troubled eyes. 'I know, but—'

'You're thinking of how Alan McDermott accused you of taking off his leg without his consent?' she asked with understanding.

He sighed. 'Yes.' His eyes became even more troubled. 'What gives a surgeon the right to play God?'

'You're not playing God,' she told him, aghast that he should think so. 'You assessed the situation and acted in the patient's best interest.'

'Yes, you're right.' His eyes cleared. 'Thanks for putting it into perspective,' he said gratefully. 'You have hidden depth, Heather Langley.'

'Did you get any sleep?' she asked, wanting to hug

him but restraining herself. Their emotions were controlled now, but it just needed a spark.

'No.'

'That's why you're thinking like this—you're tired,' she said briskly. 'And you've been working all morning?'

'Well. . .' He shrugged.

'I bet you've not even had your lunch,' she guessed, concern showing in her eyes.

'No, I've had too much to catch up with.'

'You must go right now and eat,' she told him severely. 'We can't have you collapsing.'

'I've a clinic in a quarter of an hour,' he said, a smile of amusement touching his lips.

'You stay there,' she told him firmly. 'I'll bring you some sandwiches and coffee.' He made to rise, but she pushed him back into his seat. 'No.'

'I didn't know you could be such a bully.' His smile broadened.

'I can when it's needed,' she said firmly.

'Steel behind that kind smile,' he said, a touch thoughtfully.

'When the occasion demands it,' she told him, turning in the doorway. 'Did you think I was a soft touch because I wear duck slippers?' Now why had she said such a daft thing? she thought.

Scott laughed. 'I like your duck slippers.'

'I'll give you a pair for your birthday.' She grinned.

'I'll hold you to that. It's in December.'

Heather glanced at his feet. 'What size shoe are you?'

'Nine.' His lips were twitching. 'Do you think you'll be able to find a pair that big?'

'Nothing is impossible if you try hard enough,' she

said as she turned away, deciding that now was a good time to leave him before he thought she was a complete idiot.

When she returned to the office he was sprawled in the armchair with his legs stretched out, one black-socked ankle crossed over the other. His eyes were closed and in repose the lines on his face had softened, making him look even handsomer.

Even in duck slippers he'd look good, thought Heather, her heart giving a lurch. I think the time has come to cool the relationship. It's getting too complicated. I'll have a heart attack if it keeps racing like this every time I see him.

As she placed the tray of sandwiches and coffee on the desk it clinked and he opened his eyes.

'Thanks,' he said, hauling himself upright and crossing to the desk to seat himself in front of it.

'Would you like sugar?' Heather asked.

'No, thanks.'

Peter came in at that moment. 'Scott hasn't had any lunch and no time to get any so I made him some sandwiches,' Heather explained.

'Yes, and very grateful I am, too,' Scott said, smiling up at her with his old smile and taking a bite.

'I'll just go and see how Colin is,' she said, eager to escape.

'Right.' Peter nodded.

As she left the office she heard Scott say, 'Let's have a look at Colin's chest X-ray again.'

Heather could always rely upon her work to distract her from any personal problems, and her feelings for Scott were becoming a great big one. Concentrating on comforting sick people somehow soothed any miseries she had. Her devastation after her fiancé had broken their engagement had been helped in this way.

She went into the side-ward. David Curtiss was standing beside the bed.

'How are you, Colin?' Heather asked with a reassuring smile as she picked up his chart.

'OK, I—suppose,' the young man said with some difficulty.

'I was just going to ring for you,' David said in a low voice. 'I'm not happy about him.'

Colin was a slim young man of twenty-eight, who looked about eighteen. His hair and complexion were fair, his face thin and pinched at the moment. His arms were on top of the covers, bruising making them look blue. An intravenous infusion was running.

'Have you noticed anything?' asked Heather sharply, glancing at the chart and noting recent shallowness of the patient's respirations recorded there.

'Within the last few minutes he's been experiencing pain and difficulty in breathing.'

Heather took another look at Colin and noted how blue his lips had become in just the short time she'd been there. She handed David the chart and approached the bed. 'Just going to give you some oxygen to help you to breathe,' she told Colin as she slipped on the mask and turned on the oxygen. 'Don't be alarmed,' she reassured him with a smile. 'Mr McPherson will be here in a minute.'

She hurried from the side-ward and crossed to the office.

'Something's wrong,' Scott said as soon as he saw her expression.

'I think so,' she told him. 'Colin's having difficulty

breathing and is looking blue. I think he might have a collapsed lung.'

'Right.' Scott rose with alacrity, all traces of tiredness gone. 'Let's see if you're right, Staff.'

He turned to Peter, but before he could speak Peter said, 'I'll lay a trolley in case. We always keep a sterile pre-packed chest drain here. This has happened before.'

Scott nodded his approval. He and Heather went into the side-ward. 'Hallo, there, Colin,' he said, smiling reassuringly. 'I hear you're having a bit of pain in your chest.'

'Yes,' Colin murmured.

Scott looked at Colin's chest, noting how the windpipe had moved slightly to the left—away from the side where the ribs were broken.

He then sounded Colin's chest with his stethoscope. As he returned it to his pocket he said, 'Well, you seem to have a little air where you shouldn't have, and it's caused your lung to partially collapse.' He added, before the anxiety in Colin's eyes could deepen, 'We'll soon have it out. Just give you a local aneasthetic, like you have at the dentist, so you won't feel the needle we put into your chest,' Scott explained.

'What happens then?' Colin asked with difficulty, his eyes still anxious.

'We'll attach a piece of tubing to it. The other end of the tube goes into a sealed bottle, out come bubbles of air and your lung revives.'

Scott had made it sound so simple that Colin relaxed, and he was not aware of how serious the emergency was.

David came with them to the door. 'It's tension pneumothorax,' Scott said urgently, but softly enough for the patient not to hear.

They left the room and met Peter in the corridor, push-ing a trolley. 'Tension pneumothorax, probably caused by one of his fractured ribs. No time for an X-ray to confirm. I'll put a needle in now. We'll give him an injection of diamorphine to relax him and for the pain.' Scott told them the amount he wanted given.

'David, you take the trolley in while Staff and I get the injection,' Peter ordered.

Quickly Peter and Heather checked the diamorphine and recorded it. Within seconds they had returned to the side-ward.

Their patient was even more breathless and blue-looking. Heather gave the injection while Scott washed his hands and Peter, with David to help him, prepared the patient.

There was no time for a gown. Scott injected a local anaesthetic into Colin's skin over the area he thought the collapse was situated.

He put on gloves, which Heather had tipped out on top of the trolley, while the injection took effect, then he made a small cut and inserted an intercostal self-retaining chest drain into the pleural space. The other end of the drain went into an airtight drainage bottle which had the required amount of sterile water in the bottom to provide a seal. Immediately bubbles flowed and Colin's breathing eased quite quickly.

All the medical staff smiled. 'I'll write him up for a chest X-ray,' Scott said.

David stayed to continue specialling the patient but the rest of them returned to the office, where Heather removed the tray so that Scott could write up the notes.

She was washing his dishes in the ward kitchen when he came in. 'Congratulations, Staff,' he said, giving her his heart-breaking smile. 'You're not just a pretty face.'

This stabbed at her professional pride, and suddenly she remembered him telling her she had hidden depth. Did he think she was a scatty, dumb blonde? She was furious. 'Is that how you see me?' she asked angrily. 'As a dizzy redhead? In that case, let's end this farcical relationship now.'

His remark had been said in jest, but her reaction inflamed him. 'That's OK by me,' Scott said, the smile slipping from his face and his eyes flashing as angrily as hers.

Heather swept past him and back into the office. 'I'm going off duty now,' she told Peter tersely.

He raised his eyebrows in surprise. Heather was usually so polite. 'Had a tiff with the boyfriend?' he asked.

'Yes,' she said angrily. 'I never want to see him again.'

'That's going to be a bit difficult, isn't it?' Peter said, looking anxious.

Heather knew Peter was thinking that it might affect the smooth running of his ward.

'You don't need to worry,' she said stiffly. 'It's what we both want.' And she left him abruptly.

She shouldn't be miserable—she should be pleased, Heather told herself as she jerked on her outdoor clothes in the staff changing room. I was going to end it, anyway.

But the thought of not seeing Scott other than professionally saddened her. She forgot that the physical attraction between them was the reason for her decision and just remembered how much she had enjoyed his company.

CHAPTER EIGHT

DURING the next week Heather didn't see much of Scott, and when she was on duty they treated each other with cool politeness.

She was looking forward to the return of Thomas Blacklock the following week. It would mean that Scott wouldn't be on the ward as much as he was at present when he was combining the registrar's job with the consultant's.

It was her weekend off. On Saturday morning she was busy knitting an ear for a small teddy she was making for Len's stall at his church's Christmas fair.

Gavin came into the lounge, his jeans crushed, his jumper creased and his hair awry. He sank into his armchair and groaned. 'I'm never going to attend another leaving party,' he said, leaning forward to put his elbows on his knees and clasp his head in his hands.

Heather put her knitting down on her lap and flexed her fingers. 'You look as if you slept in those clothes,' she said, smiling at his tousled appearance. 'Whose leaving, and how come I wasn't invited?' she asked.

'Well, it wasn't exactly a leaving party—just an excuse for a booze-up,' Gavin said, his voice muffled in his hands. 'Will's moving to Men's Medical.'

'What?' Heather had always liked Will. 'He didn't tell me.' She was hurt.

'Yes, he did, but you probably didn't pay attention—

any more than you did when I told you I was taking his place.'

'I would definitely have remembered that,' Heather said, affronted. She jumped to her feet in anger, her knitting falling to the floor. 'Anyone would think I was a dizzy redhead, the way you talk.' The fact that Scott had made no effort to disabuse her of the accusation still rankled.

Gavin raised bloodshot eyes to his sister. 'You're not a dizzy redhead—just a mildly dizzy one,' he said humorously.

'Thanks a bunch,' Heather said crossly. 'Anyway—'

Gavin interrupted her. 'I expect the split with Scott—'

'Has nothing to do with it,' Heather lied. She just couldn't banish him. Everywhere she looked she seemed to see him—in her bathroom mirror, in her dreams— just everywhere. 'I'm very busy, with Christmas coming and Len's Christmas fair to knit for.'

'So why are you so upset?' he asked, giving her a disbelieving look.

Heather picked up her knitting. 'Because you made me so cross. And look what you've made me do.' She planked herself down and held up the needle, from which the knitting had slipped off.

'I. . .' Gavin was going to protest, but his sister's tense face stopped him. 'Look, I heard something at the party I think you should know.'

Heather was trying to pick up her stitches. 'Well?' she asked tersely. 'What did you hear?'

'Thomas Blacklock isn't coming back. Scott McPherson is to be the new orthopaedic consultant.'

'Oh, is he?' Heather said, unimpressed. 'That'll please him.' And it pleases me, she thought as she kept her eyes on her knitting. I won't need to feel guilty now that he lost the other consultancy. 'Another step nearer a professorship.' Her tone was waspish.

'Is that what he wants?' Gavin asked.

Heather did glance up at him then. 'Don't quote me,' she said sarcastically. 'I just suspect he does.'

She gave up trying to knit and pushed the needles into the wool, before putting the knitting away in her bag.

'I'm off for a shower,' Gavin said.

Heather nodded and went into the kitchen. She could hear her brother singing in the shower and envied his carefree lifestyle.

As she filled the kettle Heather wondered if she had really been so wrapped up in herself that she hadn't listened to what people had told her.

She recalled one or two instances now when Peter had had to repeat something he had said, and remembered his exasperation at having to do so.

It's all Scott's fault, she thought illogically as she spooned coffee into two mugs. He should never have suggested a mock relationship.

It was then she remembered how surprised she'd been when he'd suggested it. He didn't seem the sort of man who would care what people said about him. Perhaps he had just been kind. That was in character.

I'll have to pull myself together, she thought, and put Scott right out of my mind. He wasn't going to become involved with a nurse, and even if he did it wouldn't be this nurse. He thinks I'm too scatty. Definitely not professor's wife material.

Suddenly a vision of herself in duck slippers, ushering his guests into dinner, made her smile and the thought helped her to squash a pang of heartache.

Heather was pouring boiling water into two mugs when the phone rang. 'Coffee's in the kitchen, Gavin,' she called as she went to pick up the receiver.

'Hallo, Heather. Glad I caught you in.'

'Hi, Uncle Gavin,' Heather said delightedly.

'Lovely to hear you're back from London. Was it very gruelling?' she asked sympathetically.

'A murder case is always trying,' he said briefly in a tired voice. 'Especially when you're defending.'

Heather's Scottish grandparents were dead so her uncle was her only relative in Edinburgh and a great favourite with her. He was her mother's brother, an eminent Queen's Counsel and much in demand.

'How long are you going to be here this time?' she asked, just as her brother came in with the mugs of coffee on a tray.

'Maybe for good,' he said in a cheerful tone.

'Are you retiring?'

'No. I've got a promotion,' he said cheerfully. 'I'm to be made a judge. You're the first to know. I haven't even told your mother yet.'

'How wonderful,' Heather enthused.

'It is, but. . .' His voice was sad.

'You wish Aunt Katherine could have shared the honour,' she finished for him. Her aunt had died two years ago.

'You always were intuitive, Heather,' he said softly and then, after a pause, added more brightly, 'A party is being given in my honour at the Balmoral on December the twelfth. Could you partner me?'

All Heather could think of was that it was Scott's birthday. She pushed these thoughts aside and mentally checked her off-duty. 'No, sorry,' she said regretfully.

'I'm on duty and can't break it.' She had already changed to oblige Peter, who wanted that evening off.

'Well, would you be able to host a party for me to repay this one?' he asked.

Heather remembered the parties her uncle and his wife had given in the past. They had been huge successes, but since Katherine's death he hadn't bothered to entertain.

'But I don't know how to,' she protested.

'Of course you do,' he said with confidence. 'You always helped Katherine, and we'll get caterers in for the food.'

It was true. Heather had always helped and had enjoyed it. 'What about the guest list?'

'I'll get my secretary to do that. I really need you to brighten up the place. The house seems so dark now that Katherine's light is no longer there.'

Heather heard the catch in his voice and quickly said, 'Of course I'll do it, always providing you choose a day when I'm off duty.'

'I'll certainly do that,' he promised.

'OK. I'll wait to hear from you. D'you want to speak to Gavin?'

'Yes, please.'

Heather handed the receiver to her brother. 'One Gavin to another,' she said with a smile. Talking to her uncle had cheered her up.

Heather had finished her coffee by the time Gavin rang off. 'Hope I'm off duty for that do,' he said.

'You'll have to see what you can do,' she told him.

The rest of the day she went Christmas shopping, and Sunday was spent wrapping presents and writing cards.

'I don't know how you can be so organised,' Gavin said, slumped in his chair.

'I have to be,' she said shortly. She cut a piece of Sellotape and fastened it to one end of the parcel she was wrapping. 'I know we send all the patients home we can, but we still have to make Christmas as good a time as possible for those who are left—and that means decorating the wards.'

Gavin nodded.

'And there's the hospital Christmas panto, remember.' She put the finished parcel aside and took another one.

'Don't remind me,' he groaned. 'I must have been drunk to agree to play one of the ugly sisters in *Cinderella*.'

Heather laughed. 'No, you weren't. I volunteered you.'

'What?' Gavin made a lunge at her, upsetting all her parcels as he did so.

Heather leapt to her feet and dodged behind the couch, laughing. 'I knew you wouldn't do it if you were asked.'

'Who made you the casting director?' He sank onto the couch.

'I'm not. I have the leading-lady role,' she said, pretending to preen herself as she came and sat beside him.

'You mean you're to play Prince Charming?'

'I'm Stafferella.'

'Stafferella? What d'you mean? I thought it was Cinderella.'

'It's a skit on *Cinderella* about a poor staff nurse who's put upon by two ugly ward sisters and is rescued by a handsome prince of a doctor.'

'And who's to take that part?'

There was a pause, then she said quietly, 'Scott McPherson.'

'Can't you get out of it?' Gavin asked quickly, his eyes sympathetic.

'And what excuse could I make?' she asked shortly. '"I'm sorry I can't play opposite Scott because we've stopped seeing each other"?' She added, 'It was a mutual parting, anyway.'

'Well, perhaps as he's to be the new orthopaedic consultant he'll cry off himself,' Gavin suggested. 'It wouldn't really go with his status.'

'Perhaps he will,' she said dully, 'but I don't really care.' Which was not true. Heather was dreading playing opposite him. It would rouse all those deliciously unwelcome feelings. She straightened her shoulders, which felt as if they were sagging. 'By the way, rehearsals start tomorrow.'

'I'm on duty,' he said with a grin.

'That's good. It means you'll definitely be in the hospital and can spare a few minutes to find out what you have to do.'

'I suppose I'll have to give in gracefully, then,' Gavin said in a martyred voice.

'Good.'

'Who's the other ugly sister?'

'Peter,' she told him.

'Are only the orthopaedic staff acting in this show?' he asked in surprise.

'No, just you, me, Peter and Scott,' she said. 'Oh, and David. He's Buttons.'

'Who's taking the part of the good fairy?' Gavin asked, becoming interested.

Heather grinned. 'The senior nursing officer, Mrs French.'

Gavin laughed uproariously.

Heather arrived on duty on Monday morning with a cheerful face, determined to banish Scott from her mind and her dreams. The fact that her brother was starting as orthopaedic houseman that morning also raised her spirits.

The ward was reasonably quiet. Colin Watson had been moved from the side-ward and was in the bed next to Michael. His chest drain was out and his pelvic fracture was confirmed as being only minor, with no sacroiliac joint damage. Scott's fears that it might not have shown up on X-ray had been groundless.

'Heard the news about Mr Blacklock not coming back and Scott taking his place permanently, Heather?' Peter asked when the rest of the staff had left the office to go about their duties.

'Yes, Gavin told me.'

'Well, at least we know Scott and what he likes,' Peter said in a resigned voice.

'I thought you were looking forward to Mr Blacklock's return,' Heather said, surprised at how meekly Peter was taking the news.

Peter looked up from his seat at the desk. 'I might not agree with all Scott McPherson's methods but it's the patients who are most important and he's an exceptional doctor.'

Heather just nodded. 'What would you like me to do?' she asked.

'Perhaps you would just get on with supervising

the ward,' Peter said. 'I seem to have a pile of paperwork here.'

'Right.' She was about to leave him when he said, 'Andrew Carmichael's coming in to have his soft tissues repaired and tightened. That'll stop his shoulder dislocating so often.'

'He'll be glad of that,' Heather said. 'He was getting fed up with having his shoulder put back repeatedly.'

'Well, he has Scott McPherson to thank for him being admitted,' Peter told her. 'He saw Andrew in Outpatients and decided the poor man had had enough.'

'Good.'

Heather liked Andrew Carmichael. He was a big bear of a middle-aged man with a jolly laugh. His injury had been caused when he'd been involved in an accident some time ago where he had fallen heavily, causing his shoulder to dislocate.

Heather had the ward work organised—temperatures taken, patients' charts recorded properly, any problems noted to tell Peter, any dressing supervised—before she made a general check on the ward so that it was ready for the round.

'Do you think I'll get out for Christmas?' Colin asked as she was tidying Michael's bed.

Heather turned round. 'That will be up to Mr McPherson,' she said, smiling kindly.

'You can't go and leave me here on my own, Colin,' Michael said. He had cheered up considerably since Colin had been put in the bed beside him. Although they were nine years apart in age they found they had much the same tastes in pop music and sports and supported the same football team.

'Patients in hospital have a great time,' Heather said.

'The nurses come round carol-singing, the consultant carves the turkey and Father Christmas comes as well.' She didn't add that the visitors were given tea in case Michael's parents couldn't come.

'I'd rather be at home,' Michael said in a small voice, then he brightened. 'Except I wouldn't see Sandra then. She's on duty.'

'We'd all like to be home for Christmas,' said a voice at Heather's elbow.

She swung round with a smile. 'This is my brother, Dr Gavin Langley, who is the new houseman,' she said, introducing him.

'Hi!' said Michael, shaking Gavin's outstretched hand. 'I didn't think of the doctors and nurses not being able to be with their families.'

'So we're all in the same boat,' Gavin said with a grin. Taking Heather by the arm, he drew her away. 'Just came to tell you Scott will be here in a few minutes.'

'Thanks.'

One of the nurses was showing Andrew Carmichael to his bed as they passed.

'Hi, Staff. New boyfriend?' Andrew asked with a grin.

'No, just my brother,' she explained, introducing Gavin.

'Tough luck,' Andrew said. Gavin was an attractive man.

They pushed both ward doors open and were laughing together when they met Scott with Peter, coming out of the office. 'I would appreciate it if you were ready for the ward round, Dr Langley, and not gossiping with your sister.' Scott's tone was terse.

'He wasn't. . .' Heather was about to protest Gavin's innocence, but Scott gave her a look that silenced her.

It wasn't so much the frown on his face that struck her dumb as the severity of his expression. It seemed harder than was warranted. It made her feel cold, and she paled.

'I expect my houseman to be on time, and with me,' Scott said brusquely, looking at Gavin.

'I apologise,' Gavin said in a suitably humble tone.

'And please keep your staff in control, Charge Nurse.' Scott looked meaningfully at Heather as he rebuked Peter. 'I am not as lenient as Mr Blacklock.'

Why was he so cross with everybody, and especially me? wondered Heather as he swept into the ward with Peter and Gavin.

She hung back for it took her a few moments to recover from the shock of his extreme displeasure. Scott had been cool since their break-up, but never like this. Surely her laughing happily with Gavin was not the cause?

But that was exactly the reason. Heather didn't seem to be missing him. Scott was irritated that she was happy while he was fighting a desire to crush her in his arms.

They had reached Andrew Carmichael's bed. 'Ah, Mr Carmichael.' With an effort, Scott smiled at the big man. 'We'll repair those torn soft tissues and tighten them up so that your shoulder won't keep dislocating whenever it feels like it.'

The staff all gave weak smiles. 'I think I explained that you won't be able to move your arm as it'll be held to your side by a bandage, but you will be able to move your fingers.' Scott looked to see if Andrew understood and when he saw that he did he continued, 'You will have a suction drain in for a day, maybe two. It depends on how much is coming out.'

'And when will I be able to move my shoulder?' Ian asked.

'We'll see how you get on. When we think the time is right the physiotherapist will start gentle exercises, which she will help you with, so as not to undo all the good work we have done.' He smiled again. 'Then, over the next few months, they will be increased. OK?'

'Yes, thanks, Doctor. It's a good job I'm a computer operator. At least I'll be able to type with one hand.' He grinned.

Scott nodded.

The rest of the round was uneventful, and when they left Gavin held the ward door open for them all to pass through.

The anaesthetist was waiting for them in the office. 'Go with Dr Taylor, will you, Heather, please?' Peter asked, handing her the notes for those patients who were for operation on Wednesday.

'Certainly,' she said, accepting the folders, only too glad to escape. Scott seemed to fill the office and, alas, her heart.

All the time she assisted the anaesthetist as he examined the patients she wondered how she was going to cope at the rehearsal that evening.

CHAPTER NINE

HEATHER needn't have worried about how she'd face Scott that evening as he wasn't there when she arrived.

Seats were grouped in a semicircle on the stage of the lecture theatre, where the meeting was to be held and the panto performed.

'Perhaps Scott's given up the part,' Gavin whispered in her ear as he sat beside her.

Heather shrugged. Let's hope he has, she thought, though a little sadly when she remembered how they'd laughed as they'd accepted the parts.

The senior nursing officer, Helen French, was the co-ordinator, as well as taking the part of the good fairy. 'One of the junior doctors has written the script,' she said as she sat in the chair placed opposite them. 'As you are all aware, it's a medical skit on *Cinderella* and has been vetted to remove the more outrageous comments.' Here she gave Neil Mackay, the author, a wry look. Everybody laughed while Neil tried to look chastised, but he couldn't keep his face straight and grinned.

Helen French was tall and slim with a refined face and greying fair hair. 'I want to make it quite clear that there is to be no ad libbing.'

Everybody groaned. 'But that's part of the fun,' Gavin objected.

'Perhaps,' Helen said. 'But sometimes it's taken too far and we're hoping to raise money for the paraplegics sports fund, and patients and relatives will be in the audience.'

The door behind her opened at that moment and Scott came in. He was still wearing the grey suit, white shirt and university tie he had worn on the round. He was as immaculate and as handsome as he had been when Heather had last seen him.

You would never realise he had been busy all day, thought Heather as a terrible longing swept over her. Only the deepening of the lines of his face, showing tiredness, betrayed him. Was the responsibility of his position the reason he seldom smiled these days? Heather asked herself.

'Sorry I'm late,' he said. 'Had to see an emergency at the last moment.'

'Don't apologise, Scott,' Helen hurried to say. 'It's good of you to take the part.' She looked at him anxiously. 'Are you sure you still want to do it? I know your time must be even more fully occupied now.'

'Hospital pantos and revues are usually great fun,' he said. 'I wouldn't miss it.' Which was a lie, he thought wryly. The last thing he wanted was to play opposite Heather, but he had promised to do the part and he didn't break his word. 'I hope we're going to be allowed to ad lib,' he added, giving Helen one of those smiles that melted Heather.

'Well, I had said that perhaps it wouldn't be a good idea as families will be present,' she said doubtfully.

'I see.' He nodded. 'Well, perhaps you're right.'

The expression on the faces of those taking part had swung from delight to resignation at his words.

'Mind you, I'm sure a little leeway would be all right, Helen, don't you?'

'It would be a pity to spoil the fun, wouldn't it?' she agreed, responding to his charm. 'Providing everyone is careful not to offend.'

'Oh, we will, we will,' they chorused.

'If you would just take a seat, Scott.' Helen gestured to the only empty chair, which was on the right side of Gavin. Heather was sitting on her brother's left.

It was strange how, now that Scott was a consultant in his own right, the staff were not as at ease with him. Heather had noticed it on the ward round.

'Gavin.' Scott nodded, acknowledging his houseman who gave him a strained smile. He ignored Heather.

Helen came forward and handed them each a script. 'This evening is just to give you these so that you can read them and familiarise yourself with your lines, then we can discuss everything next time.'

There was a rustle of paper as they flicked through the script. 'Anybody want to say anything?' Helen asked.

Scott stood up. 'I would like everyone to behave towards me as they did before I became a consultant.' He smiled generally, skimming over Heather. 'After all, I'm still the same man,' he said, before sitting down again.

Oh, no, you're not, thought Heather, annoyed with herself that she should care that he had treated her as if she weren't there. You're small-minded. She wouldn't admit to herself that she hadn't smiled at him either.

The slight tension his arrival had brought vanished from all faces except Heather's.

'The costumes shouldn't pose a problem as you can just use what you normally wear except, of course, for the ugly sisters.' They all laughed. 'We'll try and get you something that will fit, but it might be difficult.' She frowned and her blue eyes were troubled.

'If they're a bit skimpy and tight-fitting it should make it funnier,' Gavin said.

'I expect you're right.' Helen was looking even more alarmed. 'Past experience of hospital revues where some of the costumes were outrageous makes me worry a little,' she confessed.

'I'm sure we'll all consider the hospital's reputation,' Scott said soothingly.

'For putting on risqué shows?' Gavin asked cheekily.

'For using good taste when it's for a worthy cause,' Scott said quietly.

Gavin looked suitably subdued.

'Well, if that's all?' Helen looked round. 'The next rehearsal will be on Friday. I hope you can all come.'

Scott joined the senior nursing officer, and as Heather and Gavin piled up the chairs Heather was near enough to hear Helen say, 'I'm glad you're still taking part in the panto. It will keep the more adventurous quips to a minimum.'

'I couldn't very well break my promise just because I've gone up the ladder,' he said, giving her a gorgeous smile.

'No, but I thought it might be a bit awkward. ...' She was too embarrassed to finish the sentence.

'Heather, you mean?'

'Yes,' Helen said apologetically.

'We were always only friends,' he said. 'The hospital grapevine made more of it than there was.'

Eavesdropping, instead of paying attention to what she was doing, caused Heather to place the chair she was putting on top of two others to fit awkwardly, and the three chairs fell over, tipping Heather with them.

'Are you all right?' Scott asked as he hauled her to her feet, his eyes showing his concern.

His fingers seemed to burn into her flesh. 'Yes, thank you,' she said curtly, and pulled her arm away so quickly that she flinched with pain.

'I'd leave you to your brother's tender care,' Scott said tightly, 'but I have more experience in orthopaedics.'

He was treating her like a patient when she wanted more, much more. She wanted him to hold her in his arms and kiss the pain away.

'I'm sure my brother can cope,' she said loftily.

She looked so much on her dignity that Scott wanted to laugh. 'I'm sure he could,' he said more gently, 'but you are a member of my ward staff, so may I?'

Heather gave him her wrist less than graciously, and Scott examined it carefully.

Gavin, who had been putting his collected chairs on another pile, reached her. Putting his arm round her, he asked in a concerned voice if she was all right.

'Just a bit of a bruise,' she told him, though her wrist was painful.

'I think you should have an X-ray,' Scott said, looking at Helen who had joined them.

She nodded. 'You do look a bit pale, Heather,' Helen said. 'Are you sure you're all right?'

'It's just shock.' Heather was feeling sick and wobbly.

Scott lifted one of the chairs from the pile. 'Sit here and put your head between your knees,' he said gruffly.

Tears gathered in Heather's eyes. It wasn't so much because her wrist was hurting but because Scott's coldness towards her on the ward had affected her more badly than she had admitted to herself and his kindness to her now, even though he treated the patients in just the same way, was too much.

She put her head between her knees so no one would see her tears, but she wasn't quick enough for Scott. Try as he would to hold back, he couldn't bear to see her cry.

He knelt beside her and put his arm around her. 'It's probably only a sprain, but that can be just as painful as a broken bone,' he said sympathetically.

'Now is not the time to remind me I was the cause of your accident,' Heather said peevishly, pain and the desire to snuggle closer into his arms making her cross.

'I wasn't,' Scott protested angrily, letting her go abruptly and jumping to his feet. 'I was being sympathetic.'

It was as if they were the only two there. It was Helen asking. 'What accident?' that reminded them they were not alone.

'It's nothing,' Scott said in a tone that did not invite further questions.

'I'll take you to X-Ray,' Gavin said, helping Heather to her feet.

'We both will,' Scott said, wondering why he'd said he would. There was no need. Gavin was perfectly capable, but Heather looked so forlorn that Scott felt he just couldn't leave her.

'Well, you're in good hands, Heather,' Helen told her, 'so I'll go.'

Scott pulled off his tie and was preparing to use it as a sling. 'I'll just put my hand under my arm to support it as far as X-Ray,' Heather said.

'Right.'

She felt like a prisoner under escort between the two men. When they arrived at X-Ray Scott filled in a form and she was taken almost immediately.

'Thanks, Scott,' she said, and hurried to add, 'Gavin will look after me now.'

'No, I'm staying,' Scott insisted. He felt powerless, held in an emotional grip. It was as if some other Scott was speaking. 'If it's broken you'll need it set.'

Was he concerned for her, or was it the professional speaking? Heather wondered, searching his face. He had seen her look and returned it blandly.

When she came back Scott was on his own. 'Your brother was called away,' he said. 'How's the arm?'

'Just a bit sore,' she told him.

An uncomfortable silence spread between them for they were too aware of each other for it to be companionable.

'Our acting together in the panto won't bother you, Heather, will it?' Scott asked abruptly.

'No, of course not,' she said sharply.

'Good.'

He patted her on the shoulder. Just as you would praise a dog, Heather thought, but before she could think of something caustic to say he rose. 'I'll see what the X-ray has to tell us,' he said, and left her to simmer.

Scott was back in a moment. 'No broken bones,' he said briskly. 'Sister will put a Tubigrip support on your wrist and I'll stand in for Gavin while he takes you home.'

'Thanks,' she said coolly.

Sister came in just then. 'I'll fetch Gavin,' Scott said stiffly, and hurried away.

Good riddance, thought Heather, using anger to deny the bereft feeling she had.

By the time the Tubigrip had been applied Gavin had

arrived. Heather thanked the sister and they went into the corridor.

'Good of Scott to stand in for me,' Gavin said, putting his arm round her shoulder as they walked towards the exit.

'Yes,' she agreed wearily.

Hearing the doleful tone in her voice, Gavin tightened his arm round her shoulders. 'You've a day off tomorrow so have a rest.'

She did, but her wrist was quite painful. During the morning the SNO phoned to tell her to take a few more days off, but Heather insisted she could do light work. 'Well, we are short-staffed but only light work, Heather.'

She agreed.

When Heather reported for duty on Wednesday morning Peter glanced at the Tubigrip. 'I heard. The SNO phoned and said we were to treat you gently.' It was his little joke.

Heather smiled. 'I can take temperatures and do paperwork. I'm not completely useless.'

They were in the office, and Peter was standing beside the desk. 'Well, if you're sure.'

'You tell me what you want me to do and I'll do it.'

'Well, if you could check the medicine cupboard to make sure we aren't running short,' he said. 'I meant to do it yesterday but didn't have time. And take the temperatures. Nurse Richards is doing the medicine round. Perhaps you would check them with her.' He thought for a moment. 'And you could check the premeds.' He smiled. 'In fact, there is quite a lot you can do.'

'Good. I like to be busy,' Heather told him, but didn't add that it would take her mind off Scott.

'Mr Hugh Jones will need his pre-med at nine,' Peter

said. 'He's about the only patient on the list who's looking forward to his operation.'

'Looking forward to getting some pain relief for his arthritic knee,' she said sympathetically. 'He's comparatively young, really.'

'An accident in his youth is the reason,' Peter said. 'And as a heavily built man his knee has borne more strain.'

'Well, dividing the bone close to the joint in an osteotomy will give him some relief from pain, won't it?' she asked.

'Yes,' Peter agreed.

'I'd better get on with some work, then,' Heather said.

'Indeed you had.' Peter nodded.

As soon as Heather went into the ward Michael shouted, pointing towards her arm, 'Isn't that taking empathy too far?'

The other patients laughed, as did Heather. 'I just did it to get out of work, but. . .' She shrugged. Her comment raised another laugh.

Heather did a few jobs, then checked Hugh Jones's pre-med for David and went with him to the patient's bedside. 'Jones isn't a Scottish name,' she said with a smile, hoping her attempt at light conversation would relieve the tension she saw in Hugh's eyes.

'No, I'm from Wales,' he said, his birthplace obvious from his accent. 'I married a Scottish girl and came to live up here, and have never regretted it.'

David gave the injection. 'I didn't feel that,' Hugh said with a smile.

'David is our hospital darts champion,' Heather said with a straight face. 'So he gets plenty of practice.'

Hugh looked at her, then realised she was joking and

laughed. 'You can join our team any time,' he told David.

She stopped beside Andrew Carmichael's bed. 'It won't be long now,' she told him with a smile. 'We'll soon be giving you your pre-med.'

'Can't be soon enough for me,' Andrew said. 'What a relief it will be not to have my shoulder slipping out.'

'Yes, it will be,' Heather agreed.

The morning continued, with the routine work fitting in smoothly with the comings and goings of the patients for Theatre.

It was nearly her lunchtime, and Heather was looking forward to it so that she could rest her wrist, when she saw a patient, Kenneth Ogilvie, nearly fall and rushed to catch him.

He was a young man of twenty-five, who had broken his leg while learning to ski on the dry ski slope at Fairmilehead on the outskirts of Edinburgh. The bone had not broken the skin so the fracture was a closed one, the opposite to a compound fracture where the skin was broken. He had had it reduced under a general anaesthetic and a full leg plaster had been applied.

He had been measured for crutches, which the physiotherapist was bringing today.

One of the other patients had lent Kenneth his crutches, which weren't the right height, and only Heather's prompt action prevented a fall.

'You were told to wait for the physiotherapist, Mr Ogilvie,' she told Kenneth severely, helping him to hop back to his seat.

'Sorry, Staff.'

'A weight-bearing plaster will be applied in a month's time, but until then you must use crutches and they have to be the right height for you,' she explained.

'I just thought I'd have a shot,' Kenneth said ruefully.

'Well, you could have landed yourself back in Theatre if you had fallen,' she told him.

'Sorry, Staff.'

He looked so crestfallen that she relented. 'The physiotherapist will be here any moment,' she said kindly.

'Thanks.'

Heather's wrist was aching badly after this, and she felt a bit sick. She went into the office, intending to sit for a moment—knowing Peter was in the ward checking the last patient who had just returned from Theatre.

She had just sat down when Scott came in. 'You're as white as a sheet. What are you doing on duty?' he barked, his concern making him brusque.

He's being nasty to me again, she thought, tears filling her eyes. 'There's nothing wrong with me,' she snapped weepily. 'It's not as if my wrist is broken, and we're short-staffed.' She sniffed. 'Everything would have been all right if Kenneth Ogilvie hadn't nearly fallen and I had to catch him.'

Scott drew the other chair close to her and, sitting down, put his arm round her shoulders. He was wearing theatre greens and she could feel his warmth though them and smell the scent of his soap. That traitorous desire flared again. Heather hid her face in his shoulder so he wouldn't see it.

Scott handed her a tissue from the box on Peter's desk. 'Kenneth's a bit big to catch, isn't he? I'd concentrate on balls if I were you,' Scott said, hoping his little joke would make her smile.

Heather raised her head, leaving a damp patch on his shoulder. She looked so charming, smiling through her tears and with her red hair curling about her cap, that

Scott couldn't help himself. His grip tightened and he
kissed her gently on the lips and wiped her eyes, just
as he would have a child. It took iron self-control to
release her.

Oh, why did he have to do that? wailed Heather to
herself as she tried to subdue the fire his kiss had started.
First he treats me like a pet dog and now he's treating
me like a child—when all I want is for him to treat me
like a woman. Thoughts of her broken engagement and
memories of Bill had all flown away. Scott filled her
world. What a time to discover she was in love with him.

'Oh, go away,' she said, the enormity of the revelation
making her cross.

'Now, then, Staff Nurse Langley.' Scott's tone was
soothing. 'You're to go off duty this moment.'

'But. . .'

He leaned towards her. Heather thought he was going
to kiss her again and she felt she couldn't cope with
that, knowing—as she did now—that she loved him. She
might betray herself.

Much to her relief, it was only his finger that touched
her lips to stop her protest. 'No buts. Let's have a look
at your wrist.'

He gently removed the Tubigrip but, even so, Heather
had to bite her lip to stop crying out with the pain. 'Brave
girl,' he said, looking at her approvingly. His praise
cheered her, but then he added, 'You're not going to
faint, are you?'

'Of course not,' she told him fiercely, her anger sweep-
ing the threatened faint away.

'Good. It wouldn't do for me to strain my back, lifting
you from the floor,' he said with a straight face as he
gently examined her wrist.

Her anger at him implying that she was overweight distracted her from her pain. 'I'll have you know I'm not that heavy.'

He was crouching beside her and looked up with a grin. 'I'll remember that if you do faint.'

He had been teasing her in order to distract her, she realised, and she smiled a little tremulously.

He rose to his feet. 'I think a crêpe bandage would be better,' he told her. 'I'll fetch Peter.'

'N—' He was gone before she could object.

Scott came back with Peter. 'Heather!' Peter said. 'You should have told me you were in pain.' He looked at her swollen, bruised wrist with concern.

'I'm fine,' she said swiftly. 'It's just Scott, making a fuss.' She rose to her feet, but sudden dizziness made her sway.

Scott pushed her gently back into her seat. 'I'll phone the SNO,' he said. 'If that's agreeable with you, Peter?'

Heather smiled in spite of the pain in her wrist. Scott was becoming more diplomatic.

'Fine by me,' Peter hastened to agree. 'I'll get you a cup of tea, Heather.' He hurried away.

Scott was only a few moments on the phone. He finished his conversation with, 'I'll see to that, Helen.' The receiver clicked as he replaced it.

'See to what?' Heather asked sharply.

'See to you being taken home,' Scott told her.

'I'm perfectly capable of seeing myself home,' she said curtly.

Scott's eyes smiled with amusement. 'I'm sure you are, but we must make sure you get home safely.'

Peter's arrival with the tea prevented her from giving

a caustic reply, but her eyes showed her thoughts and Scott laughed.

'You're feeling better?' Peter asked solicitously as he handed her the mug, handle first. 'Careful, it's hot,' he told her.

Another one treating me like a child, thought Heather. She wasn't cross with Peter but, then, she wasn't in love with him.

'I just came to check on Andrew Carmichael, Peter,' Scott said.

'He's fine.'

'Good. I'll go and change, then.'

Scott left them.

Heather felt better after her tea. Peter returned with a crêpe bandage and applied it to her wrist. 'Keep it up as much as possible—that'll reduce the swelling, as you know,' he said kindly.

'I will, Peter, and thanks.' He opened the office door for her. 'Sorry to let you down like this.'

'You haven't,' he assured her. 'If you hadn't been there Kenneth would have fallen.' He smiled. 'You go home and rest that wrist.'

Gavin came into the office. 'Scott said I'm to take you home,' he said. 'Try and have lots of accidents, then I'll get plenty of time off to look after you.' He grinned.

'I can't promise that,' she told him. 'It's just lucky for me that you're Scott's houseman.'

She said goodbye to Peter and left with her brother.

As the taxi drove them from the hospital she thought how glad she was that Scott had decided not to drive her home himself.

CHAPTER TEN

HEATHER'S wrist improved rapidly. She was off duty for over a week and during that time she went to visit Len and Janet.

'Sorry I can't do any more knitting,' she told them ruefully, 'but I can serve behind a stall on Saturday as long as I don't use this hand.'

'We can put you on the same stall as Scott,' Janet suggested.

'Is he helping?' Heather asked, a bit aghast.

'Didn't you know?' Janet was surprised.

Heather hadn't told her friends about the split.

'Scott and I aren't seeing each other now, except at work,' she explained evenly.

'Oh, I'm sorry,' Janet said quickly. 'You looked as if you were made for each other.'

'I'm sure Heather doesn't want to discuss it,' Len said, sensing her distress.

'Oh, it doesn't matter,' Heather said airily. 'It's mutual.' And she explained why they had been thrown together.

'I see,' Janet said brightly. And she did see. She saw that Heather was in love with Scott, but she changed the subject. 'How about being on the ticket table at the door with Len?'

'Fine.'

*   *   *

It was Saturday morning. 'You're up early,' Gavin said with a yawn as he came out of his bedroom into the hall, where she was putting on her anorak.

'It's Len's Christmas fair today,' she said. 'How about lending us a hand later?'

'I have other plans. Anyway, Scott's helping,' Gavin said. 'He's on call for any emergency.' He ran his hand through his tousled hair. 'Is he giving you a lift?'

'No. I'm taking the bus.' She was looking around for her bag. It wasn't there. Heather pushed past him and went into the lounge. It was on the floor by her chair. 'I must go.' She gave her brother a quick kiss as she rushed past him. 'See you later.'

Heather hoped she hadn't missed the bus, but it was just leaving the stop as she turned the corner. She was standing, fuming, when Scott's car drew up beside her. He leaned across and opened the passenger door. 'Gavin told me you'd probably missed the bus when I called for you.'

'You didn't need to bother,' she said a bit stiffly. 'And there'll be another along in a minute or two,' she told him.

'Better Saturday service than on my route, then,' he said wryly.

'Quite a few of the buses run past the hall,' she told him.

'So I take it you don't want a lift?' He sounded impatient.

'No, thanks.' Sitting beside him in the close confines of the car would kill her. 'A bus is just coming and you're parked at the bus stop.'

He shrugged and slammed the door shut. 'OK,' he said in a couldn't-care-less tone. She could see him muttering to himself as he drove off.

Heather climbed aboard the bus and as she looked unseeingly out of the window she told herself she must be strong. It was no good hoping Scott would fall madly in love with her. Full of this resolve, she managed to greet Len and Janet cheerfully and even smiled at Scott.

As the time passed Heather noticed that Janet looked worried and came to check on Len often.

When the first rush of people had finished and only one or two were coming for tickets Heather said, 'Are you all right, Len?'

'I upset a cup of tea on my leg and Janet wanted me to go to the doctor's, but I insisted on coming here.' He gave a rueful smile. 'It's not as if I feel any pain.' There was no self-pity in his tone.

'No, but you know how important it is,' she said seriously.

'Yes.' There was a touch of impatience in his tone. 'Janet is always checking on my skin for bedsores.' He sighed.

Heather had never seen him so despondent. 'Shall I fetch Janet?' she asked kindly.

'No, Heather. I don't want her to see me like this.' He took in a deep breath. 'It passes. Sometimes my lack of independence aggravates, that's all.' He shrugged. 'That's why I insisted on coming here instead of going straight to the doctor's.'

'I know it's silly to say I understand when only some- one who is in your position can really know what it's like, but I can empathise.' She gave him one of her sweetest smiles.

Scott and Janet came up behind them. Scott had heard

the sincerity in Heather's voice and seen the smile, and he groaned inwardly.

He had hoped, when they'd split up, that he would be able to dismiss her from his mind and just treat her as a colleague.

She was inclined to be scatty, she confused him and she was a nurse—which was against his relationship rule. But when he saw her sweet smile, felt the warmth that emanated from her, saw how the patients loved her and knew how much she cared for everyone he felt drawn even more to her. And that wasn't even counting the physical attraction.

'Janet told me about your burn, Len,' Scott said, forcing himself to concentrate on Len.

'You shouldn't have bothered him, Janet,' Len said impatiently. 'Your treatment is OK.'

'I just thought I'd mention it.' Janet's tone was a bit terse. 'I don't want it to get any worse.'

The anger left Len's eyes and he reached for her hand. 'She looks after me so well,' he said softly. 'And I repay her with anger.' There was remorse in his tone.

Janet bent to kiss him. 'It's because I love you, no matter what,' she said simply. 'I don't care that you're in a wheelchair as long as I have you.'

'It's true, you know,' said Len, once more his cheerful self. 'Love does conquer all.'

Tears brimmed in Heather's eyes. To be loved and to love like that—then she realised that that was how she loved Scott.

'I think we should take you home and have a look at your leg,' Scott said.

'OK. When we've finished here,' Len agreed.

'No, now,' Scott insisted.

'I'll be here,' Heather said. 'Just you and Janet go. I'll call round and let you know how much money we took.'

'Thanks,' said Len.

The rest of the morning passed quickly, with Heather serving one-handedly on the stalls as best she could. The fair raised five hundred pounds, which delighted them.

She was helping to clear up when Scott came back. 'Oh, I didn't expect to see you,' she said, her heart doing its usual flippity-flop.

'Nice to be wanted,' he said sarcastically.

Now why did he speak like that? wondered Heather. You'd think he was disappointed at my reception.

'Wanted?' she said. 'Of course you're wanted. Wanted to lift some of these heavy boxes.' And she grinned to hide just how much he was wanted, but not to move boxes. I bet his love-making moves mountains, she thought, having to stop herself from drifting into fantasy land.

The sardonic expression left his face and he laughed. 'Show me where.'

As Heather took him over to the boxes she asked after Len. 'I had a look at his leg and it's not too bad so I phoned his GP and gave him the details,' Scott told her. 'Janet's quick treatment had prevented it from becoming worse.'

'Yes, she's very efficient and has plenty of equipment for emergencies, but I can guess how she must feel,' Heather said compassionately. 'It's so different when it's a loved one who is hurt.'

'Yes.' He gave her an intent look. 'I can understand that.' He realised now how much her fall had disturbed him. Of course that was just concern for a patient, he tried to convince himself.

Scott helped move the heavier things. 'You're going to Len's, if I remember correctly,' he said. 'I'll give you a lift there if you've finished.'

'Thanks, but I have some shopping to do first,' she told him, which was true, though she could have done it later.

'OK, I'll see you when you're back on duty,' he said, but didn't turn away.

'Was there something else?' she asked, wishing he would go and wondering why he was looking at her so thoughtfully.

'No.' He shrugged and left her.

Heather did some shopping to salve her conscience and then, feeling she couldn't face Janet's and Len's silent curiosity, she phoned them to tell them about the fair's takings. Janet answered and was delighted.

'I must go now,' Heather said. 'My uncle's expecting me.'

'Oh, yes,' Janet said. 'His cocktail party tonight.'

'Yes. It's just about organised.'

'Good.'

Heather rang off. She had a quick sandwich at a snack bar, then caught the bus to her uncle's.

She was glad she had something to occupy her because she missed her knitting. She rang her uncle's door bell and was let in by the resident housekeeper. Margaret Gregson was a homely woman in her early sixties. She had been with the family for years.

After she'd sympathised with Heather about her injury they joined her uncle in the lounge.

'Tough luck about your wrist,' he said sympathetically.

'It's almost better,' she told him.

'When do you go back to work?' he asked.

'Monday.'

They discussed final arrangements and then she left.

Heather had bought a new dress for the occasion. The lines were simple and black flattered her figure. She had meant to have her hair cut, but had been too busy.

That evening she showered and dressed, pleased to have finished with the Tubigrip. As she brushed her hair until it gleamed and her curls bounced on her shoulders, she swung her head from side to side and decided to keep it that length. I can pin it up for work, she thought.

A light make-up without lipstick did nothing to tone down the healthy glow of her skin. She surveyed herself in the mirror and was pleased. No one would think I'm pining for that gorgeous man, she thought with a toss of her head.

A black jacket, shoes and bag completed her outfit.

Gavin was waiting for her in the lounge. 'Wow!' he said, his eyes gleaming with admiration. 'You look great.'

'It's the new dress,' Heather said. 'You don't look so bad yourself.' She walked round him. 'I don't remember seeing you look so smart.' His grey suit fitted him perfectly and his white shirt—usually he wore coloured, casual ones—and his university tie made him look a different person.

'It's the new suit,' he said, his eyes alight with laughter—glad she seemed more like herself.

'About time.' She eyed him critically. 'You'll do, except. . .' She frowned. 'Except for the tide-mark on your neck.'

'Tide-mark?' He rushed to the mirror to check. His neck was spotless. She had teased him. He swung round, to find her laughing. 'If I wasn't all dressed up I'd tickle you,' he said threateningly.

As neither of them had a car they travelled to their uncle's in a taxi. Mrs Gregson let them into the large hall. Black and white tiles lined the floor and a curved staircase swept up one side. The hall had an appearance of a bygone age.

Gavin senior came out of the study. 'You two make a handsome couple,' he told them as the light fell on them. 'Leave your jacket in the spare bedroom, Heather,' he told her.

Heather ran her hand up the curving banister rail as she went up to the bedroom and sighed almost happily. She'd always liked being in this house. It had an air of contentment which made her feel at ease. She'd never been able to decide if it was the house itself, and those who had left their aura from the past here, or the graceful presence left by her aunt which was responsible.

Her brother and uncle were standing with glasses of whisky in their hands before the imposing, though not ostentatious, marble mantelpiece when she joined them.

As Heather accepted a sherry she looked with satisfaction about the large room. The trouble she and Margaret had gone to had been worth it. The dark, old-fashioned furniture had been polished until it gleamed. The beige covers from the armchairs and couch had been washed and replaced, and scatter chairs had had their woven seats brushed.

Red velvet curtains, hanging either side of the two bay windows, gave a feeling of warmth, to which the muted red and beige design in the carpet added. Flowers in bowls were everywhere—on the occasional tables and the grand piano, which was loaded with family photographs.

Gavin senior put his arm round Heather's waist.

'Thank you, Heather,' he said softly. 'The room looks as graceful as it always did when Kate was alive.'

'That's because she taught me so well,' Heather said brightly, to offset the sadness she heard in her uncle's voice.

He smiled. 'You're a good girl, Heather.'

They had just finished their drinks when the first guest arrived.

An hour later Heather slipped out to the kitchen to make sure there were enough canapés.

Returning with a plate in her hand, she nearly dropped it when she saw Scott. What was he doing here?

Her astonishment was reflected on his face. 'Moon-lighting?' he asked with amusement, looking at her black dress.

'Ah, Scott.' Gavin senior joined them. 'I'd like to introduce you to my niece, Heather Langley, who is responsible for all this.' He smiled affectionately at Heather. 'She makes a charming hostess, don't you think?'

'Indeed she does,' Scott agreed, rather surprised. Heather was looking anything but scatty. 'We already know each other. Heather is the staff nurse on my ward.'

'Of course. Orthopaedics,' Heather's uncle exclaimed. 'Here, let me take that.' He took the plate from Heather and left them.

'What are you doing here?' Heather asked bluntly. If only she had checked the guest list she would have been prepared.

'I treated your uncle in London when he broke his arm,' Scott said. 'He remembered when he invited my brother who was in his legal department.'

'I forgot your brother was in the legal profession.'

He didn't take her arm as he had so often in the past, and she was grateful. She could do without her body leaping into life just now.

'You seem to have a lot of talents I don't know about,' he said as they moved across the room.

'Yes, I'm not just a pretty face,' she taunted him.

'You're not going to let me forget that, are you?' he said, smiling down into her upturned face.

He seemed more relaxed this evening, more approachable. 'I might,' she quipped, thinking how wonderful it would be if he would wrap his arms about her and kiss her to bits.

'Well, thanks.'

They were laughing when they joined his brother, who was talking to a blue-eyed, sophisticated, blonde woman. 'My brother, Callum, and his partner, Rosemary,' Scott said, introducing Heather.

Callum was considerably younger than his brother. 'Charming,' Callum said, smiling down at her, but his smile was insincere. He looked very astute and a bit brittle, as did Rosemary. They seemed well suited. 'You must give me your phone number.' He made it sound suggestive.

She wanted to say, 'Not on your life,' but just smiled faintly and hoped it wasn't too sickly a smile.

Good manners made her stay for a moment or two longer, then she said, 'I'm afraid I must go. Can't leave my uncle in the lurch.'

'You can't let this charming lady escape, Scott,' Callum said, catching hold of Heather's arm.

'Stop flirting with my girl,' Scott said quietly, seeing the look of distaste Heather was trying to hide.

'I was only teasing,' Callum said quickly, letting

Heather go. He had heard the steel in his brother's voice.

'He's like that with all the women he meets,' Rosemary said smoothly. 'It means nothing.'

It might mean nothing to you, thought Heather, but I find it offensive. She slipped away. Scott's girl, indeed, Heather thought as she rubbed her arm.

'Sorry about that.' Scott apologised for his brother as he caught up with her. 'He thinks he's irresistible.'

'Think nothing of it,' she told him airily. He looked as though he was going to detain her, but she hurried away.

Heather was kept busy, seeing to the welfare of their guests. As she flitted from person to person, making sure no one was left looking lonely, she was aware of Scott's eyes following her.

Eventually the party began to break up. Heather was at the door to see people out. Rosemary and Callum, with Scott behind them, approached her.

'We've said goodbye to your uncle,' Rosemary said in a bored tone. 'Lovely party,' she drawled.

'Callum has something to say to you,' Scott said sternly.

'Oh, very well,' Callum said sulkily, with a glare at his brother. 'I'm sorry, Heather.'

He didn't look a bit contrite. 'I've had to fend off much worse in Casualty,' she told him sweetly.

Callum gaped, while Scott grinned.

'Oh, do come on,' Rosemary said impatiently, catching hold of Callum's arm.

Scott was about to follow them when Heather put her hand on his arm to hold him back. 'Why did you tell your brother I was your girl?' she snarled.

'He's such a woman-chaser that I thought it would stop him pestering you,' he said easily. 'But I needn't have bothered, judging by your answer just now.' He grinned. 'You can certainly take care of yourself.'

Heather was disappointed, and her expression showed it. She wanted to be his girl—wanted it very much.

As she made to turn away Scott caught hold of her and pulled her into the cloakroom. 'Oh, to hang with it,' he said gruffly.

His arms went round her and he started to kiss her to bits, just as she'd longed for him to do. When he released her she was too breathless to speak. 'There,' he said huskily. 'Now you are my girl.'

'You don't have to be such a caveman about it,' she managed faintly. 'You only had to ask.'

He took her face in his hands. 'Well, I'm asking nicely. Will you be my girl?' His tone was soft, seductive.

'Even though I'm a nurse?' she whispered.

He kissed her again, this time gently. 'I don't care if you're Florence Nightingale.' He kissed her very thoroughly. 'I'm fed up with fighting this urge.'

'Is that what this is? Just an urge?' Heather demanded, pulling her lips from his as he made to kiss her again.

'No, Heather,' he said softly. 'It's more, much more.' He released her. 'I'd better go,' he said huskily. 'Before your charms overwhelm me and I forget I'm a gentleman.'

Forget, forget, she cried, but the words didn't pass her lips.

They crept out of the cloakroom like naughty children, big smiles on their faces.

'Goodnight, Heather,' Scott said, the expression in his eyes leaving her in no doubt that he was fond of her—but did he love her?

CHAPTER ELEVEN

HEATHER spent a restless night, waking frequently to wonder if she had dreamed that Scott had told her she was his girl. She slept later than she usually did and woke to find herself twisted in the duvet. As she struggled to unravel it she fell on the floor, fortunately not damaging her wrist.

What would happen now? she wondered as she made herself tea and toast for breakfast. Gavin was still in bed.

As Heather went about the household chores and filled the washing machine her mind went round and round.

She was in love with Scott, but was he with her? Heather longed for him to make love to her, but knew how that longing would deepen when he did. She remembered the agonising nights she had lain awake after Bill had broken their engagement, and was determined that it wouldn't happen again.

Seeing him socially would be different this time. It would be because they both wanted it, but was he only interested in an affair? Heather knew she wanted more, a positive commitment, and that meant marriage.

She was just putting the duster away when the phone rang. 'It's Scott for you,' Gavin called, having dragged himself out of bed to answer it.

Her heart started to hammer. Now, then, she told herself, use your head. Gavin's bedroom door closed as she went into the hall and picked up the receiver. 'Hello,' she said, and was proud of how calm her voice sounded.

'It's such a nice day I thought you might like to go to Peebles.'

'Oh, I'd love to,' she said eagerly. 'It's one of my favourite places.'

'OK. I'll pick you up in ten minutes.'

Heather was wearing old jeans, an old sweater and her duck slippers. She rushed to her bedroom. Where are my black jeans? she thought frantically. They're in the wash, along with all my other good clothes, she answered herself. Why did I decide to have that big wash today? she agonised.

Botheration. Rummaging in her wardrobe, she found a pair of jeans which had been cast aside because they were too small. I hope they fit, she thought as she pulled off her old, tatty ones and squeezed herself into them.

Now I know how those poor women felt, laced into corsets, in the old days, she thought. Glancing at herself sideways in the mirror, she realised the jeans were too tight everywhere. A long jumper's the answer, she decided.

She only had one and it was red. Some reds she could wear, but not this red.

The doorbell rang at that moment. Och, why am I making such a fuss? she thought as she pulled them on. What could she wear on top that would be long enough to cover the jumper?

Again she searched and dragged out an old anorak patterned in red, blue, orange and green. She'd had it for years and had thrown it into the back of the wardrobe. It would cover the jumper better than her leather jacket, though. Catching up her shoulder-bag, she slung it onto her shoulder and left the room.

Scott was waiting for her in the hall. His eyebrows

rose at her strange outfit, but he made no comment.

Seeing his expression, Heather thought, I expect he's decided I'm not suitable for the vacancy of professor's wife. Instead of being mortified by this, it struck her as funny and she grinned.

'Some sort of test?' he asked, raising his eyebrows.

'Pardon?' She gave him a puzzled look.

'We're going to a fancy dress party instead of Peebles?'

'What are you talking about?'

'Your clothes.'

Heather looked down at them. 'What's wrong with them?'

'Nothing. Forget it,' he said too quickly.

'I suppose I do look a bit bizarre,' she said, and assumed a serious expression, deciding to tease him. 'But quite colourful, don't you think?'

'Yes.' A humorous glint touched his eyes.

Heather relented. 'The fact is I had a big wash day and so all my good clothes are too damp to wear.'

Scott laughed.

'So you only have yourself to blame,' she said pertly.

'How?' He looked confused.

'If you'd said at the party that you wanted to go out today I wouldn't have put my good jeans in the wash.'

'I was waiting to see what the weather was like,' he explained.

'You'll just have to take me like this or make another date,' she said, more cheerfully than she felt. She wanted desperately to go out with him.

'I'll take you,' he said, grinning. Then he straightened his face as he added, 'But perhaps you'd better put on some dark glasses.'

'Dark glasses?' Was he being serious? Her expression showed what she was thinking.

Scott couldn't keep his face straight any longer and laughed.

He was teasing her now. 'You can go off people,' Heather said, joining in his laughter.

'Come on.' He put his arm round her shoulders.

'Bye, Gavin,' she called, and received a muffled reply from his bedroom.

The sun was shining weakly in a blue sky. It was cold, but the heater in Scott's car was efficient.

They took the Penicuik road. 'Let's take the turn-off for Auchendinny,' he said. 'It'll bypass Penicuik.'

'Good idea,' she agreed.

Heather was intensely aware of Scott's closeness in the confines of the car. It brought with it a feeling of well-being, of wanting to stay in the car for ever. She had the insane desire to lock all the doors and not let him escape.

Heather marvelled at how quickly they were in the countryside. It was one of the things she liked about living in Edinburgh.

The road took them through the small village of Auchendinny until they reached a crossroads at the Leadburn Inn. Looking ahead, she could see the hills and took a deep breath.

'Yes, I love it, too,' Scott said as he turned left onto the road that would take them to Peebles. 'You feel free up here, don't you?' He glanced sideways into her sparkling eyes.

'Yes,' she agreed. 'Absorbing such beautiful scenery renews the spirit.'

He nodded in agreement. 'The peace from being up

here helps us to go back and do our jobs, where we see so much pain.'

Heather was thrilled that he thought as she did. 'You understand.'

'Yes,' he agreed simply.

The road wasn't busy and within half an hour they turned into the car park at Peebles. She climbed out and Scott locked the doors.

'Do you want to look at the shops?' he asked.

'Not really,' she told him. Heather wasn't too interested in clothes, unlike most women. 'I'd rather go for a walk along the river.'

'You're the first woman I've met who doesn't drag her man into every shop,' he said, with an amused twinkle in his eye.

Her man, Heather sighed, but was he really her man? 'Well, you've a bargain in me,' she said, smiling up at him.

Scott linked his arm in hers as they walked into the high street with its Tontine Hotel and the church at the end of it.

They took a side way down to the river. An area of grass with houses on two sides lay before them. A road bridge crossed the river, but they took the foot bridge to reach the path on the other side.

'If I'd known you didn't want to shop we could have parked in that car park,' Scott said with a smile, gesturing towards the car park on the side they had crossed to.

'You don't know me very well,' she said a little shyly.

'That's something I intend to remedy.' He stopped to give her a bear hug, but Heather stiffened in his embrace. 'Hey! What's wrong?' He gave her a concerned look.

'Nothing, really,' she told him, though she didn't smile.

'I'm going too fast for you,' he said in a decided tone.

'Well. . .' She paused. How could she put her feeling into words? She wanted to know where she stood, but didn't know how to ask him. It was rather a leading question—are your intentions honourable?

He smiled gently, guessing something of her problem. 'I want to see more of you, Heather,' he said softly, then grinned cheekily. 'Much more of you.' His inference was clear and she smiled. His expression became more serious. 'And this time it's not because of the hospital gossips.' She was still in his embrace. He tipped her chin up with his finger and kissed her gently. 'That OK with you?'

It was the 'much more of you' that bothered her, and he hadn't said he loved her. Think with your head, Heather. 'Yes, but let's take it easy,' she said. 'I've had one disappointment and that makes me wary,' she told him honestly.

'Oh, yes. I was on the receiving end of that,' he said, and laughed. 'Just you tell me the man's name and I'll go and break his leg.'

Heather grinned.

After that she relaxed and they walked and talked, hand in hand or with arms linked—but she liked it best of all when he put his arm round her shoulders. Her shyness left her and the friendliness they had shared before returned.

They had lunch in a hotel, choosing soup for the starter, poached salmon for the main course and a sticky chocolate gateau as a sweet. Coffee followed.

Heather was so happy she hardly knew what she ate.

Scott drove her home and went with her up to the flat.

'Would you like to come in for coffee?' Heather asked, a little nervously because she knew her brother wasn't at home.

'Too soon, isn't it?' Scott's tone was gentle. 'But perhaps a kiss?'

For answer, Heather twined her arms about his neck and kissed him in gratitude. But it wasn't gratitude that made her respond so eagerly, nor was it the strong attraction between them. It was love.

Scott pulled her arms from around his neck. 'That's not fair,' he said huskily. 'A man has only so much self-control.'

'I was just testing it,' Heather quipped.

'Take a tip from me and don't test it too often,' he advised, and grinned.

'I'll try and remember that,' she said, putting her arms round his neck again. 'But you're so. . .'

Scott wiggled his eyebrows up and down. 'Handsome. . .clever. . .'

'Conceited, more like it.' She gave him a playful punch on the jaw, then became sober. 'I was going to say kind, approachable, lovable. . .'

'Hey! Hey!' he interrupted her. 'I really will become conceited if you go on like that.' He kissed her gently, then released her with a sigh. 'I'd better go.' It was said reluctantly.

Heather suspected that only a word of encouragement from her would make him stay. She was tempted, but resisted the temptation.

'Goodbye.' He didn't kiss her again but left, and she could hear his footsteps going down the stairs—they sounded cheerful.

* * *

Heather had dreaded going back to work, but now she arrived on duty early on Monday morning with a smile on her face.

After the report had been given Peter kept Heather back and sent the rest of the staff about their duties. 'Had a good weekend?' he asked.

'Mmm,' Heather murmured, her eyes dreamy.

'I see you've got another reason for not concentrating now,' Peter said drily.

His words brought her back to earth. 'What reason?' she asked, frowning in puzzlement.

'Must be another man in your life to make you look so radiant,' he said.

Heather just grinned.

'Have a seat, Heather,' Peter said, gesturing to the chair beside the desk where he was sitting. 'I'll brief you on the patients you don't know,' he said. 'Eric McInnes.' He rose and drew the case-note from the trolley. 'Crush injury to right hand.' Compassion filled his eyes as he resumed his seat. 'Scott tried to save it, but he had to amputate.' Peter shook his head. 'Such a shame. Eric was an up-and-coming violonist, but now. . .'

'What a pity,' Heather said sadly. 'How's he taking it?'

'He appears to be taking it very well, but I don't know.' Peter frowned. 'I don't think the implication of it has sunk in yet and neither does Scott so we decided it would be better for him to be in the side-ward for a couple of days.'

'What makes you think his acceptance isn't genuine?' Heather asked.

'He's too uptight, too brittle and he won't see his girlfriend.'

'I see.' Heather nodded.

Peter's face cleared. 'Perhaps you'd like to see what you can do,' he said. 'If he'd only cry—or be angry.'

'I'll try,' she promised.

'Michael's going to Theatre today to have his Steinmann's pin removed.'

'Right.'

Peter told her about another two patients, then she left him.

Heather went about her duties, the smile fixed firmly on her face. She didn't think anything could remove it, but she was wrong. She felt it slipping the moment she entered the side-ward and saw Eric.

She had opened the door quietly and so caught an anguished expression on his face which vanished as soon as he saw her.

'Hi,' Heather said, hiding her compassion behind a bright smile. 'I'm Staff Nurse Langley.'

'Oh, yes,' Eric said, looking up at her with eyes that were too bright. 'You hurt your wrist, didn't you?'

'Yes.'

'It's better now, though?' he asked evenly.

'Yes, thanks,' she told him.

Always sensitive to people, her profession had developed this aspect so that she saw the suffering behind the bright eye and the cheerful tone.

How could she help this young man who was sitting beside his bed, his back straight, his head up? The courage in his eyes defied her to pity him.

He had a sensitive face, finely drawn, with blue eyes and fair hair. His build was slim, which made him look younger than his twenty-seven years.

Now that he had regained his strength perhaps shock tactics were the answer. He wouldn't take sympathy.

What he needed was something to shake him out of this awful world of horror he was in.

'I'm certainly luckier than you are,' she said brightly. 'I've still got my hand.'

Eric gaped. Everyone had been so sensitive to his loss since the accident and here was this nurse. . .

'Call yourself a nurse?' he shouted. 'How can you be so insensitive? I've lost my whole world.' And as he admitted it tears gathered in his eyes and his head sank forward.

Heather had tears in her own eyes as she rushed to put her arm about his slumped shoulders. He stiffened and tried to pull away, but she clung to him. 'You're alive,' she whispered. 'And when the shock of this loss is over you will rise again.' Her tone was positive.

Heather felt his warm tears on her arm. She let him cry himself out and when he raised his head she handed him a tissue and said, 'I believe you write music—that's a great gift.'

She was only guessing, but it proved to be a good guess.

'How did you know?' he asked, all his anger draining away.

'All musicians do, don't they?'

'You're not insensitive,' he said quietly. 'You spoke like that to make me see things as they really are.'

Heather just gave him a hug. 'Feel better now?' she asked, worried in case she had been too brutal.

'Much.' He looked relieved. 'And. . .thanks. You should be a psychiatrist.'

She laughed. 'No, thanks.'

Heather went into the treatment room and leaned against the sink with her head bowed, feeling completely drained. A moment later the door opened behind her, but she didn't turn round.

An arm came round her shoulders. 'Are you all right?' asked Scott gently.

Heather turned in the circle of his arms and snuggled closer. 'Why is life so cruel?' she asked, the tears she'd held back flowing onto his white coat.

His arms tightened. 'You're thinking of Eric,' he said quietly, holding her away from him. 'I've just seen him.'

Heather nodded. 'A talented musician ruined at the start of his career.'

Scott smoothed the tears from her face with his thumbs. 'There are other avenues in music open to him, just as you told him, and he's a lot better.'

Heather pulled away from him. 'I just said that to raise his spirits, but will it last?' she asked in distress.

Scott took her back into his arms. 'It won't be easy for him but, with encouragement, he will be all right in time.'

'I hope so, for his sake,' she said, her face still drawn with emotion.

He stroked her back. 'You must try not to become so emotionally involved,' he advised her.

'I do, but it's hard,' she said, looking up at him with a troubled face. 'The best I can do is not to show the patient how affected I am.'

Scott kissed her gently on the lips. 'I know,' he said. 'It's difficult to use your head instead of your heart when your heart is moved.'

He understands, she realised. She was so involved with this thought that she didn't hear the surprise in his tone, as if he had only just realised it himself.

'Thanks,' she said with a tremulous smile.

'Any time,' he said warmly. 'Are you OK to do the round?'

'Of course,' she said quickly. 'Sorry I've taken up your time.'

'I'll always make time for you, Heather,' he said softly, looking deeply into her eyes. He loves me, she thought, her eyes glowing with the thought. 'As long as it doesn't interfere with work,' he added, with a straight face.

He doesn't love me, she decided, her happiness fading, because if he did he wouldn't make conditions like that.

She knew she was being unreasonable, but couldn't help it. Women took these things more seriously than men and she couldn't afford to make a mistake this time.

Scott had turned away to open the door for her so he didn't see the change in her expression.

They returned to the office where Peter was waiting for them. 'Can we do the round now, please?' he asked with veiled sarcasm.

'Sorry to have kept you waiting, Peter,' Scott said, but didn't explain.

Gavin burst into the office at that moment. 'Sorry to be late,' he apologised, and breathed a big sigh of relief to find the round hadn't started.

Scott frowned but made no comment.

They went into the ward. Scott stopped at Michael's bed. 'Out of traction today.'

'Yes. I'll quite miss it.' Although he joked, it didn't disguise the apprehension in his eyes.

'Don't worry,' Scott said gently. 'Think how nice it will be to turn over on your side.'

Michael's face brightened. 'I hadn't thought of that.'

They moved on to Colin Watson. Peter handed Scott the notes, opening them at the relevant page. Gavin had seen the patient, who had complained of a burning sensation when he passed urine. A urine specimen had been sent to the laboratory.

Scott flipped through the notes, but could find no report. 'Where's the report?' he asked Peter.

'Gavin. . .' Peter paused. He didn't want to get Gavin into trouble.

Heather opened her mouth, but caught Scott's eye and closed it.

'I was to collect it,' Gavin confessed.

'Well?'

'I forgot,' Gavin said in a small voice.

'Go and phone the laboratory now,' Scott said grimly. 'We'll wait here.'

'Everything all right?' Colin asked anxiously.

'We'll know in a minute,' Scott told him reassuringly.

Gavin returned quickly and told Scott the result.

'You seem to have a bit of an infection in your urine,' he explained to Colin, who immediately looked worried. 'But an antibiotic will soon clear it up,' Scott assured him.

'But will it stop me going home for Christmas?' Colin asked anxiously.

'We'll see how you get on with the antibiotic first,' Scott said, not wanting to raise false hopes.

The round continued. Scott reached Andrew Carmichael's bed. 'You'll have your sutures out in a day or two,' he said, glancing at the notes. 'I prefer them to be left in for ten days.' He gestured to the body bandage Andrew was wearing. 'And we'll be able to dispense with that soon and give you a collar and cuff support.'

'Thanks, Doctor,' Andrew said.

They returned to the office, with Gavin helping Peter

to manoeuvre the trolley through the door.

'Shall I get the coffee now?' Heather asked faintly. Scott's anger with her brother was almost palpable.

'I'm running late,' Scott said, 'so we'll just go to the female ward now. Gavin can come back and write up the notes later.' He picked up Colin's folder, opened it and wrote up the antibiotic. 'See he starts on it right away, please.' He handed the notes to Peter.

Scott stormed out of the office, with Gavin creeping behind him.

Her brother returned to the office after the round on the female ward and found her there alone. 'Phew,' he gasped, sinking into a chair. 'What a telling-off.' He looked quite pale.

'Well, you did deserve it,' she told him.

'Thought you were in my corner.' He looked quite hurt.

Although she felt sorry for him she said, 'You know how important treating a urinary infection immediately can be.'

'You sound like Scott.' His shoulders sagged. 'He said that urinary infections in pelvic injuries were a priority.'

'Did Scott know you'd worked twelve hours?' she asked gently.

'Yes. Told me it wasn't a mitigating circumstance. That where the patients were concerned there was no excuse.' He looked up at her. 'And he was right.'

'I'll make you a cup of coffee. You'll feel better then,' she told him.

'Thanks.'

When she came back with a steaming mug of coffee she found him writing up the notes. 'Thanks,' he said absent-mindedly.

The routine of the morning continued. Michael came back from Theatre in a normal bed.

When he came round from the anaesthetic he beckoned to her. 'It's so strange,' he told her when she joined him. 'I'm not looking down on people any more.'

'Yes, I suppose it must be,' Heather agreed. She hadn't thought of it like that before. 'Are you all right? Not in any pain?'

'Not at the moment,' he said sleepily.

'Good. Well, just you go to sleep.'

The rest of the day passed smoothly. Heather looked forward to seeing Scott that evening at the panto rehearsal.

But he wasn't there when they were all assembled. 'I'm afraid Mr McPherson is unable to join us.' Helen didn't explain why.

Must be work, thought Heather.

One of the 'ugly sisters' was the day sister and the other the night sister. Stafferella was on the day shift. 'Stafferella, you're to take the place of the night sister so she can go to the ball,' Gavin said in a falsetto voice as the day sister.

'But I've been on all day,' wailed Heather as Stafferella.

'Where's your devotion to duty?' he snapped. 'Twelve hours should be nothing to a nurse. The junior doctors work that many a time.'

Scott came in just as the cast shouted, 'Hurrah!' He must have heard what Gavin had said, thought Heather, aghast.

'That's not in the script,' Helen said, searching the relevant page.

'Isn't it?' Gavin pretended to look puzzled. Then he saw Scott and looked sheepish.

'No, it isn't,' she said sternly. 'And I thought we'd agreed there'd be no ad libbing.'

'Ah-h-h!' the rest cried, with big grins on their faces.

'This is a panto, not an opportunity to air your views,' Helen said. 'Now, let's get on. We'll miss out the parts that include the prince,' she said.

'No need,' Scott said. 'I'm here now, and I think you should leave that bit in about the junior doctors.'

'Well, if you think so, Scott,' Helen gave in.

There was another cheer from the cast.

The rehearsal continued. Heather found she didn't need to act opposite Scott. It came so naturally.

'Well, that's all for this evening. Do try and learn your lines,' Helen insisted.

Scott and Heather were the last to go.

It was quiet in the lecture theatre.

'That was very kind of you to suggest leaving in that bit about junior doctors,' Heather said as she looked up at him, her red hair glowing in the electric light. The pink jumper she was wearing gave her complexion a rosy glow—or was it a blush? he wondered. In her jeans she looked about sixteen and adorable.

He came closer to her, close enough for her to see the pattern of his tie. Were those ducks? she wondered.

'I was a junior doctor once,' he said. The softness of his tone drew her eyes from his tie to his face, and the expression of love she saw there melted her so that unconsciously she leaned towards him.

In a moment she was in his arms. 'Heather, Heather,' he murmured against her glowing hair. He took her face in his hands and kissed her, deeply, longingly, lovingly, so that she was transported to that seventh heaven where only he seemed able to take her.

When they broke apart Heather expected him to declare his love for her, but he didn't. 'How about coming home with me?' he asked, half-seriously.

She would have loved to have gone home with him. Loved to have made mad, passionate love, but. . . Never again would she go to bed with a man until she was married.

'No, you haven't any etchings to show me,' she told him, making a joke of it to avoid agreeing.

'I'll get some. I'll get some,' he promised eagerly with a grin, not pressuring her. Putting his arm about her, he went with her to collect her coat and bag.

'Sorry, I can't give you a lift,' he said, helping her on with her anorak. 'I want to check on one of the female patients. She's anxious about her hip replacement operation tomorrow. I just want to reassure her.'

How kind and understanding he was, thought Heather as they left the theatre.

He kissed her briefly before parting. 'See you tomorrow,' he said.

CHAPTER TWELVE

CHRISTMAS was a week away and during that time Heather saw Scott frequently—on and off the ward. He was always attentive and loving, but didn't press her for more than a kiss when they parted after an evening out. But what kisses. They always left Heather full of longing and vaguely dissatisfied. What was he waiting for? Why didn't he declare himself? She knew he loved her. Perhaps she didn't measure up socially?

Three days before Christmas the Christmas tree was decorated, glittery coloured bells were hung from the bed curtain rails and Christmas scenes were stencilled on the windows. A grateful patient had sent pots of poinsettias, which added to the Christmassy air.

'Very nice,' said Scott, admiring the ward as they entered to start the round. He stopped at Colin's bed. 'You can go home for Christmas as your urinary infection seems to have cleared up but you must continue with the antibiotic, and I want you back in again for the day after Boxing Day.'

'Thanks, Mr McPherson.' Colin smiled broadly.

Michael was now using crutches. 'I'm sorry we can't give you the same news, Michael,' Scott told him ruefully as he paused beside Michael's bed, 'but it would be too much of a risk.'

'Oh, that's all right,' Michael said cheerfully. 'I don't want to fall and break the other leg,' he joked.

'Glad you're taking it so well.' Scott was surprised.

'I'll come and visit you on Christmas Day,' offered Colin.

'You must stay with your family,' Michael insisted, rather too forcefully.

There were only two more patients in the ward. Andrew Carmichael was one. 'I think we'll let you out,' Scott told him, 'as long as you are careful.'

'Thanks.' Andrew's face lit up with pleasure.

Scott stopped at the next bed but it was empty. 'Where's John Campbell?' he asked, raising his eyebrows enquiringly.

Peter looked worried. 'I hope he hasn't skipped,' he said.

'He was here a moment ago,' Heather said, glancing up the ward, her expression as anxious as Peter's. Then her face cleared. 'Here he is.'

'Thought I'd gone walk-about?' John asked. He had the heavily lined face of an outdoor man beneath a thatch of thick grey hair. His frame was spare and he was the same height as Heather.

She grinned at him. He was a special favourite of hers, probably because his eyes were the same colour as Scott's and he had an independence of spirit that matched her own.

'How are you?' Scott asked. He was fond of John as well.

'Ready to leave here,' John said.

'Not just yet,' Scott told him gently. 'You had a bad beating and we need to keep you until you can cope.'

'I can cope now.' John sounded affronted. 'I've had worse than this.'

'You were younger then,' Scott said kindly.

'Can't argue with that, I suppose,' he admitted with regret.

'Don't you think you should think about—?' Scott started to say.

'An old people's home?' John finished for him, anger flashing in his eyes. 'No way. I've tramped the roads for years and intend to die out in the heather.' His independent spirit shone from his eyes.

'OK.' Scott gave in. 'But you must promise not to leave the hospital until you're well enough,' he said firmly.

'I give you my word as a gentleman of the road,' he assured Scott with dignity. He lifted his bruised arms and gestured at his two fractured ribs. 'None of this would have happened if I'd stayed out of the city.'

'Why did you come to Edinburgh?' asked Scott curiously, pulling forward a chair for John to sit in.

'Had a hankering to see the city again.' Affection showed in his eyes as he continued, 'In all my years of wandering—in Australia, America and Europe—I haven't found a place to compare with it.'

'I'll second that,' Scott agreed.

Peter and Heather murmured their assent also.

The round finished and they left the ward. 'Be all right if I go ahead to the female ward?' Gavin asked. 'I want to check on a patient.'

'OK.' Scott nodded. 'I'll see you there when I've had my coffee.'

They were seated in the office with their coffee when Scott said, 'Michael's taking staying in for Christmas very well.' He glanced up at Peter.

'He has a girlfriend. One of the junior nurses,' Peter explained with a smile.

'I see.' Scott laughed. 'There's nothing like love to keep you happy.' He looked straight at Heather as he spoke.

Is that a declaration of love? she wondered as she fought to keep the blush and the inane grin from her face.

'Are you going away for Christmas, Scott?' Peter asked him.

'No,' Scott replied. 'I'm having it with my family.'

'So am I,' Peter said with a smile. 'Heather has offered to do the duty. She should have been off.'

'That was very kind of you, Heather,' Scott said, a little surprised that she hadn't told him. 'Didn't you want to go home for Christmas?'

Heather had wanted to very much, but she wanted to stay near Scott more. 'The weather can be a bit tricky at this time of year for getting back,' she improvised.

'Of course,' he said, his eyes alight. 'Your family lives in the Lake District, don't they?'

'Yes.'

'Your father's a farmer, I believe,' Scott said, with a sly grin.

A grin like that meant he'd remembered how her parents had met. 'That's right.' Her eyes narrowed and she gave him a warning look.

'But your mother's Scottish, isn't she?' he persisted with twinkling eyes.

'Yes,' she said through clenched teeth.

'How romantic.' Scott's smile broadened. 'Does Peter know how they met?'

'No,' Peter replied for her, his eyes gleaming with curiosity.

'I'm sure the female ward must be waiting anxiously

for you, Mr McPherson,' Heather said quickly, glaring
at him.

'I'm not so busy this near Christmas.' Scott was
enjoying teasing her. She looked so adorable when she
was aggravated. Fire shone in her eyes.

'Well, I am,' she said, slamming the mugs onto
the tray.

'You can have a longer coffee-break,' Peter said, eager
to hear more. 'We're not busy either.'

Scott laughed. His chair scraped on the floor as he
rose. 'I'd better go before Heather breaks those mugs.'

He held the door open for her. 'After you, Staff,' he
said, his lips twitching as he gestured for her to
precede him.

'Thank you, sir,' she said with her head up, glaring
at him.

Once they were in the corridor she turned to him and
said, 'If I wasn't carrying this tray I'd punch you.'

'Lucky for me you are, then,' he said, barely able to
talk for laughing.

His eyes were so gleeful and he looked so cheeky that
it made Heather want to drop the tray and throw her
arms about his neck to kiss him. Instead, she laughed
with him. 'I didn't know you could be such a tease.'

Scott had walked with her into the kitchen. He took
the tray from her. 'There's a lot you don't know about
me,' he said and then, pushing his chest out, he added,
'Punch away.'

'And don't think I won't,' Heather said, thrusting her
chin forward but making no effort to hit him.

'Well?' Scott took a step nearer to her, his eyes alight
with amusement.

How can I hit someone I love? Heather thought. She

threw her arms round his neck and said, 'I'll squeeze you to death, instead.'

'What a way to die,' he whispered, before he kissed her.

His kiss stirred her as it always did, but she knew it would leave her wanting more so she thrust him away. She shouldn't have encouraged him but her longing to be in his arms, to feel his kisses, had tempted her.

'What's wrong?' he asked, half in amusement and half seriously.

'Nothing.' She straightened her dress. 'It's just not the right place.'

'You're right,' he agreed, but his eyes were thoughtful. At that moment his bleeper sounded. 'Oh, by the way.' Scott paused with his hand on the side of the door and looked back at her. 'My brother asked us to come for drinks on Christmas Eve.' Scott sighed. 'I know he's a bit brittle, but he's only been like that since our brother, Mike, died.' Sadness touched Scott's eyes. 'He just adored him,' Scott explained. 'So, can you come?'

'Yes,' she said gently and, standing on tiptoe, she kissed his cheek.

'Thanks.' The sadness left his eyes and they gleamed with mischief. 'Is that the best you can do?'

'At the moment, yes,' she said, not trusting the gleam in his eye.

'OK, I'll let you off this time, but not for long.' He gave her one of those devastating smiles which left her feeling weak at the knees and walked away.

His 'not for long' nagged at her for the rest of the morning. It sounded as if he was becoming impatient— waiting for her to admit him to her bed.

Peter went off duty at one o'clock.

At about three-thirty Heather was counting the sleeping tablets and found that one of the seconal capsules was missing. It didn't matter whether it was one or a hundred—this was serious. No one was written up for this sedative so someone must have taken it.

At that moment Scott came into the office. She turned to face him, her heart hammering.

Seeing her agitation, Scott asked kindly, 'What's wrong, Heather?' Concern showed in his eyes.

'I've found a discrepancy in the number of seconal capsules,' she told him.

'Oh.'

'How many?'

'One,' she told him.

'Who counted them last?'

'I did, and signed that they were correct.'

'But the night nurse would have found the discrepancy,' Scott said.

'No, she wouldn't. None of the patients are on seconal.'

'But, surely, two of you check the drugs together,' he said with a frown.

'Not the last time,' Heather said. 'I did it on my own.'

'Would you like me to count them?' he asked soothingly.

For answer, Heather handed him the bottle.

Scott drew a clean piece of white paper from the desk drawer and tipped the red capsules out onto it. They lay like splashes of paint, higgledy-piggledy.

He counted them carefully. 'Twelve. How many should there be?' He glanced at Heather and knew by her anxious expression that it was not the right number.

'Thirteen,' she whispered.

Scott looked into the small brown bottle. 'Here it is,' he said quietly. 'Stuck in the bottom.'

'Oh-h!' Heather breathed a huge sigh of relief. 'Thanks.'

Scott caught her in his arms and kissed the anxious lines from her face. 'I'm here any time you need me.' He smiled gently and when she saw the love in his eyes her heart swelled.

'I love you, Heather Langley,' he whispered, his voice rough with emotion. Then his eyes became impish. 'Even if you're only half-Scottish.'

Happiness glowed in her eyes as she leaned away from him. 'That's the half that counts, isn't it?' she whispered, almost too overcome to reply.

'What time are you off duty?' he asked, grinning.

'Not until nine,' she said.

'Right. I'll book a table at that restaurant for lovers for half past,' he said, using a mock French accent. 'At least we'll fit in with the clientele this time.'

She laughed.

They re-counted the capsules and put them back into the bottle, then they both signed the drug book.

As the door closed behind him she thought, Tonight's the night he'll ask me to marry him. Why else would he choose the restaurant where we first dined?

The rest of her duty passed in a glorious haze of happiness.

Scott was waiting for her at half past eight. 'I'll be in my office. Come along when you've finished and I'll give you a lift home.'

'Thanks,' she said, barely able to conceal her excitement.

He was leaving just as the night staff nurse came in

with the junior. The usual night staff nurse was on nights off and Karen Mackie was the relief.

'Good evening, Staff,' Scott said politely as he left.

'So it's on again,' Karen said, with a hint of envy.

'We're just good friends.' Heather used the words of the famous when they didn't want to commit themselves.

'Ha!' Karen didn't believe her.

It would be all over the hospital by morning, thought Heather, but she didn't mind. She would be engaged by then.

Heather gave the report, changed into outdoor clothes and went to Scott's office. As she knocked on his door she remembered the last time she had been there—to complain about the rumour of a relationship between them. Heather smiled happily and entered when she heard him say, 'Come in.'

Scott capped his pen and rose. 'Hey, that outfit will do—unless you want to go home and change?' He was looking at her with approval.

Since their relationship had become firmer Heather had decided to renew her wardrobe. She would need smart clothes to be the wife of a consultant so she had used money saved for a future holiday and bought a couple of expensive outfits.

Normally she came to work in jeans, but today she must have had a premonition because she was wearing smart, dark grey trousers in a lined woollen material— the weather had turned frosty—a white silk blouse and a navy blue woollen cardigan. A long navy blue trench coat, which had cost a fortune, flat shoes and a shoulder-bag of the same colour completed the outfit.

'OK, if you think I'll do.'

'Do?' He took her into his arms. 'You'd do if

you were wearing rags and tatters, my darling.'

He really did love her if he thought that! Heather returned his kiss with passion and it was he who had to pull her arms from about his neck.

'Carry on like that and I'll sweep you off to my tent.'

'Down, boy,' she said, laughing.

They left the hospital arm in arm and he seemed reluctant to let her go even to step into his car.

Trying to park was difficult. 'We should have left it at the hospital,' he said, just as a car moved out of a parking space. Quickly he took it.

As they left the car Scott put his arm round her shoulders. It was still there when they entered the restaurant, but this time it was in keeping with the atmosphere.

She took off her coat and cardigan and gave them to the cloakroom attendant. They were shown to their table—the same one they had had before. 'Did you ask to be seated here?' Heather asked Scott as he drew her chair out for her.

'Yes,' he said simply, as he rested his hands on her shoulders for a moment, before taking his seat.

Heather's appetite, which was usually so good, had left her. Must be love, she thought with a happy sigh.

They ordered the same food as they'd had the last time. Throughout the meal they spoke little but looked a lot, their eyes speaking for them.

Heather glanced at the other diners and didn't envy them. She was here with her loved one this time.

They lingered over coffee and Heather felt sure that Scott would propose now. He looked into her eyes and said, 'Will you—?'

She was so tense that she interrupted him. 'Yes.' It

was his puzzled look that stopped her adding, Yes, yes, yes, I will marry you.

'Amazing how we can read each other's thoughts,' he said on a pleased note. 'You knew I was going to ask if you were carol-singing round the wards on Christmas Eve. Amazing,' he repeated.

Amazing how wrong you can be, too, she thought, hoping her disappointment didn't show on her face. 'Yes, isn't it?' she lied.

'So you are?'

'Carol-singing? Yes.'

Scott paid the bill, and as they left the restaurant she thought, Well, there's still time. Perhaps he'll propose when we say goodnight. Her spirits soared.

'Would you like some fish and chips?' he asked as they walked back to the car, his arm round her once more.

'No, thanks.' It would choke her.

'I'll just take you home, then.'

'Thanks.'

They collected the car and within minutes were parking outside her block of flats. Now, she thought as Scott turned off the engine and took her hand.

His face was serious as he said, 'Heather, I think we should get something straight.' He turned her hand palm upwards and kissed it. 'I love you very much, but I don't believe in marriage.'

Heather saw him searching her face. In her profession she had become adept at hiding her feelings from patients so they wouldn't see how their injuries affected her. Now she used the same discipline to hide her dismay behind a bland expression.

'I've seen too many happy couples end in divorce— my parents were one of them.' He shrugged, then smiled ruefully. 'So I want you to think about our just living together.'

Heather's heart dropped. She loved this man desperately and she could understand his reasoning. She too, had had experience of friends splitting up but, to her, marriage was more than a commitment. It was a binding together. The gold ring symbolised love without end. She knew it was her romantic nature which made her see it like that, but it was something she couldn't help.

However, the thought of losing Scott was too terrible to contemplate so, as cheerfully as she could, she said, 'I'll think about it.'

'OK,' Scott said, hiding his disappointment that she hadn't agreed immediately, without having to think about it. Then he remembered her broken engagement and said sincerely, 'I won't let you down.'

Heather smiled and kissed him gently on the lips. 'I know you won't, but it's a big step.' All her dreams were clouded.

Scott stepped from the car and was round at her side to open the passenger door in a moment.

Arm in arm, they climbed up to her floor. 'Coffee?' She felt she should ask, though she really didn't want him to come in. She needed to think. 'Gavin's out.'

The muted light in the hallway lent an added softness to her features. There was a wistfulness about her that swelled his love. Had he hurt her by his request? Scott wondered. He took her in his arms and kissed her soft, responsive lips gently. 'I love you, Heather Langley,' he whispered, to reinforce his declaration.

Her face blazed with happiness. 'I love you, too,' she murmured. 'Very much.'

Her response allayed his fears and he kissed her again.

'I'll collect you on Christmas Eve at seven,' he said.

'Yes,' she whispered, part of her wishing he wouldn't go and part of her wishing he would.

Heather didn't wait to hear his footsteps tap-tap-tap down the stone steps, but entered the flat. She crossed to the window and looked down, to see him looking up. He waved and blew a kiss.

As she watched his car move away her face was sad.

CHAPTER THIRTEEN

IT WAS Christmas Eve. As the ward was so slack some of the staff had been sent elsewhere. Peter had told Heather she could have a half-day.

She hurried home at one o'clock and went straight to her bedroom. Lifting a dark green dress from her wardrobe, she viewed it critically. It was expensively cut and would be perfect for this evening. Even Rosemary would approve.

The material was brocade, but unpatterned. It had a square neck, a fitted bodice with three-quarter sleeves and a straight skirt which made her look slimmer.

Heather hoped it would fit her because she'd bought it after the split with Scott when her appetite had suffered and she'd lost weight. It had been meant for the hospital Christmas party and she had spent the money on it in an act of defiance. This will get me another man and make me forget all about Scott, she had thought at the time.

Nervously, she tried it on. It just fitted. It'll be all right if I don't breathe too deeply, she thought. She was pleased with the picture her mirror showed her of a sparkling young woman in a dress that made her look a million dollars.

Heather slipped it off, and spent the rest of the time before Scott was due to collect her having a lazy bath, painting her fingernails with a clear colour, brushing her hair until it shone and generally indulging herself.

But as she prepared herself she wondered apprehensively if Scott would ask her for an answer tonight.

By the time the doorbell rang she was ready. Opening the door, she allowed Scott to see her in all her glory, and was rewarded by him giving a wolf whistle. 'You look gorgeous,' he said, his eyes glowing with admiration and desire.

'You don't look so bad yourself,' she told him, which was an understatement.

He was wearing a dark grey, almost black suit which showed off his fair, Nordic-type skin and made his dark hair look blacker. His shirt was white which added to the impression that he was wearing a dinner jacket but the red and grey tie swept this illusion aside.

What an attractive magnetic man he was, thought Heather, suddenly feeling depressed as she wondered how long it would be before Scott tired of her. His life partner should be a confident, sophisticated woman like Rosemary.

The smile of appreciation slipped from his face as he saw the sudden sadness in her eyes. 'Something wrong?' He stepped forward to take her gently in his arms.

Heather smiled up into his face. 'No, not now you're here,' she lied.

He gave her the sweetest smile she had ever seen. 'I'm glad I make you happy,' he said softly. 'That's all I want to do.'

'Oh, Scott,' she whispered, tears creeping into her eyes.

'Hey! What's wrong?' he asked in concern.

'Absolutely nothing,' she said lightly. 'It's just that I love you so much.'

Scott gave her a light kiss. 'Come on, we'd better go.'

At that moment a group of students, two girls and two

boys, clattered down the stone steps from the flat above, their young, excited voices echoing in the sombre stairwell.

'Hi, Heather,' one of the young women said. She was about twenty and slim, with long blonde hair woven into a plait which swung as she moved.

'Hi, Kirsty.' Heather only knew the girl slightly.

'Ah, the exuberance of youth,' Scott said without envy.

Heather collected her warm winter coat and locked the flat.

Scott gestured for her to precede him. As they came out into the street their breath whitened in the frosty air, and she shivered.

Scott put his arm round her and pulled her close. 'Come on, let's run,' he said with a grin. 'The car's down the road a bit.'

She pushed herself away from him. 'Race you,' she called, already ahead of him.

His long legs could easily have outdistanced her, but he came up behind her. 'You let me win,' she accused as they both laughed.

'You've got to remember my femur's held together with a plate,' he said with a grin.

'Well, you should run even faster, being bionic,' she joked and searched his face to see if behind the grin he still blamed her, but his eyes were smiling.

As he unlocked the passenger door the students roared by in an old sports car. 'Going too fast on these roads with black ice,' Scott said grimly. He nodded towards the couple sitting up on the car's folded hood, waving their arms and singing carols. 'And that car is only made to carry two people, with one in the bucket seat.'

The street where Heather lived was lined with parked

cars, whose owners had residents' permits. Scott drove slowly, keeping a good distance between the sports car and themselves.

They were nearing the end of the street when a cat shot across the road. The sports car swerved and apparently hit black ice. The driver braked hard, throwing out the couple in the back just before the car smashed into those parked on the right.

Scott stopped and, before leaping out, put on his hazard lights. 'The mobile phone's in the glove compartment,' he said briskly. 'Phone the hospital.'

Quickly Heather did so, then hurried after him. 'You see to the couple in the road,' he told her as he examined the people in the car. 'I've given them a cursory look and they're both conscious.' His tone was tense. 'There's no smell of petrol and I've turned the engine off.'

As Heather approached the couple she recognised Kirsty, who was struggling to her feet. Heather put an arm round Kirsty's waist to support her. 'Is Duncan all right?' the younger woman asked in a faint voice, her face pale and her voice trembling.

'I think so,' Heather told her. 'I'll take you to that car, Kirsty,' she said gesturing towards Scott's Rover. 'You can sit there until the ambulance arrives.'

'But I don't want to leave Duncan,' the young woman said, her voice rising.

'Duncan's all right,' Heather said firmly, hoping she was telling the truth. 'You can help him by doing as I say.'

'If you're sure, then,' Kirsty murmured faintly.

Heather gave her a quick examination. 'I think you've broken your right arm. You must have landed on your side,' she said quietly. 'There's a graze on your face and you'll probably have lots of bruises. Does your head hurt?'

'No, just my face.' Kirsty looked anxious. 'Will I have a scar?'

Trust a woman to think of that, thought Heather. 'I don't think so once it heals. Is your chest sore?' she asked.

'A bit.'

She could have fractured ribs on her right side, thought Heather, but her breathing doesn't seem shallow so perhaps it's just bruising.

Heather was worrying about Duncan. 'Just rest and support your injured arm,' she said, lifting it gently for Kirsty to hold. A moan escaped the injured girl's lips. Heather took the rug from the seat beside her patient and wrapped it round Kirsty. 'The ambulance will be here in a moment,' she told the young woman. 'I'll let you know how Duncan is.'

She hurried over to him. The man was moaning and trying to sit up. 'Oh, my head,' he groaned.

Heather pressed him to lie down. 'Do you have any pain?' she asked as she examined the cut on his head. It was quite deep and bleeding badly.

'My head and my side hurts,' he groaned. 'And my leg.'

Heather took of her coat and laid it over Duncan, then she hurried back to the car. 'Is he all right?' Kirsty asked as Heather grabbed the box of tissues.

'I think so,' she said.

She rushed back to her patient and pressed a wad of tissues on his cut.

Heather glanced across to where Scott was bending over the other couple in the car. He must have felt her eyes upon him because he looked up. 'OK?' he asked.

She nodded and raised her eyebrows enquiringly. He shook his head slightly. Heather knew it didn't mean that he wasn't all right, but that one—or both—of his casualties was dead.

Her shoulders sagged for moment, then she braced them. Scott came across to her. 'How is he?' he asked.

Scott was so calm and assured that Heather immediately felt better. The accident had shocked her, but her training had steadied her. 'I think his leg's broken,' she said in a quiet voice. Then she gave him an assessment of Kirsty's injuries. 'I put her in the car.'

'Right, I'll see her in a minute.' Scott crouched beside Duncan. 'I'm a doctor,' he told him, before giving Duncan a quick examination. 'Looks as if you've broken your leg but we'll soon fix that. The ambulance will be here in a minute.' He smiled encouragingly. 'This young lady is a nurse and she'll stay with you.' Scott rose and put a comforting hand on Heather's shoulder. 'I'll have a look at your other patient.'

As Scott left Heather he heard Duncan ask after Kirsty in an anxious voice.

The sound of sirens came clearly across the frosty air. Heather had never been so glad to hear them or to see the flashing blue lights.

Two ambulances came, with the police following. Scott knew the paramedics and spoke to them. Very quickly the accident victims were put into the ambulances and driven away.

The police questioned Heather, and Scott told them he would give his statement later, explaining that he might be needed at the hospital.

Before he left he had a word with Heather as he handed

her her coat. 'It'll need cleaning,' he said ruefully. 'Oh, and your lovely dress.' He was looking at the blood that had stained it, and he seemed shocked.

'It'll clean,' she told him gently, touched by his concern—but what did a damaged dress matter, compared to the two deaths? Tears gathered in her eyes as she thought of the students' parents.

'You need a strong cup of tea,' Scott said, quickly pulling himself together. 'Nothing like it when you're in shock.'

Scott had reacted so strongly because he had just left another young woman whose dress had been similar to Heather's, and that young woman was dead. It had shocked him into the realisation of just how much Heather meant to him—more than life istself.

'I was thinking what a dreadful Christmas for those young people's loved ones,' Heather said tearfully.

Scott took her into his arms. He wanted to kiss her passionately, keep her by his side for ever, but restrained himself and kissed her gently. 'I wish I could take you home,' he said, 'but I'd better see if I'm needed.' He held her close and whispered, 'I don't know what I would do if anything happened to you.'

'Nothing's going to happen to me,' she told him firmly, concerned at the vulnerability she saw in his eyes. Mistakenly she assumed that his anxiety was in case she was mugged on her way home. 'The flat's just a step away and it's early. I'll have a hot bath and take your prescription of a cup of strong, sweet tea.' She smiled as she repeated his advice. 'But what about your brother?' she suddenly said.

'I'll let him know.'

Scott gave her a lingering kiss and released her

reluctantly. 'You won't be going to the carol-singing round the wards now, will you?'

Heather thought for a moment. 'Yes, I will.'

He gave her a concerned look, but didn't remonstrate with her. 'I don't think I'll make it,' he told her ruefully.

Heather walked with him to the car, then hurried home. She was starting to shiver as she put the key into the door. As a nurse she had seen the result of accident cases, but the suddenness of this one had left her unprepared.

A hot bath, a sweet drink and some food did help.

Later that evening Heather toured the wards with the rest of the staff not on duty. The nurses wore their cloaks with the red linings outside, the doctors wore their white coats and they all carried lanterns.

The effect it created brought tears to many patients' eyes. The young faces of the staff, singing well-known carols, in the muted light might have made a fanciful person see past generations of nurses walking beside them.

After they'd left the last ward coffee and mince pies were served, and an air of jollity prevailed. A group of doctors and nurses was going out afterwards. They had heard about the accident and encouraged Heather to come with them, but she refused. 'Bed calls,' she told them.

She was filling a hot-water bottle when the phone rang. It was Scott, asking how she was.

'Fine,' she said, and she was. The carol-singing had helped. 'Have you been busy?'

'A bit,' Scott said. 'You'll find that young man on the ward tomorrow. He had a fractured femur, but we were able to pin and plate it.'

'Good.'

'See you tomorrow, then, sweetheart,' he said gently.

It was the first time he had used an endearment and it thrilled her. 'I'll look forward to that,' she said happily. The click as she replaced the receiver sounded loud in the quiet flat.

The next day was Christmas Day. Heather had always loved Christmas. Her childhood had been happy and her memories of past Christmases delightful. This was the first time she had risen feeling sad, the tragedy of the crash still with her.

There was no sign of Gavin. He must have partied late into the night and slept at one of his pals' flats, Heather decided.

There were Christmas presents to open, but she had no incentive to, still haunted by the deaths of those young people. Quickly she washed, dressed and hurried to the hospital.

As she walked down the road—it was too icy to cycle—past the cars the accident had damaged her sad feeling stayed with her.

When Heather arrived on the ward David, the other nurse on duty with her, was already there.

'Happy Christmas, Staff,' he said cheerfully.

Heather pulled herself together and smiled. 'Happy Christmas to you, too.'

She discovered from the night staff that Duncan knew about his friends being killed. 'Mr McPherson told him, and so kindly,' Karen informed her. 'He's a super doctor,' she said, adding enviously, 'You're lucky.' She drew the case-note forward and flipped it open. 'The patient's still suffering from the shock of it all so Mr McPherson wanted him kept in the side-ward for now.'

Heather nodded.

As soon as the report was finished she went in to see Duncan. His pale, pinched face looked up at her anxiously. 'Tell me it was all a dream,' he said hopefully, 'and that I got this falling downstairs drunk.'

Heather put her hand on his arm. 'I'm sorry,' she said kindly, shaking her head.

Tears filled his eyes. 'He was my best friend,' he said tremulously. 'And Susan went to school with me.'

Heather felt helpless. What could she say to alleviate the pain she saw in his eyes? Nothing would bring back his friends. 'Kirsty's all right,' she told him, managing to sound cheerful. 'She's to be kept in for a day or two, but will be down to see you later.' She gave him a tissue from the box on his locker.

'That's great news,' he said, wiping his eyes.

'I'll be back in a minute,' she said.

The night staff had not left his Christmas stocking in his room, thinking he might like it later when he was feeling better.

Heather took it from the office and went back to the side-ward. 'Father Christmas left this for you,' she told him, handing him the stocking. She couldn't very well wish him a happy Christmas, considering his circumstances.

'Thanks.' The dullness in his eyes lifted for a moment as he drew soap, face-cloth and comb from the sock. 'Just what I need,' he said, meaning it.

'How's the pain?' she asked.

'Not too bad.'

Heather didn't believe him. She had seen the tension in his face and the pain in his eyes that was not due to the loss of his friends.

'I'll get you something for it,' she told him.

Heather found Scott in the office. 'You're just the person I want,' she told him.

'Really?' His eyes lit cheekily and he reached for her.

'Oh, no, you don't,' she said laughingly as she dodged out of his grasp. 'Duncan has pain and I need someone to check his analgesic.'

'Right.' Scott's face became serious. 'How is he?' he asked as he checked the drug and signed his name.

'Upset,' she told him as she washed her hands, collected the syringe, snapped off the ampoule top and drew up the injection.

'Bound to be,' he said, watching her closely. 'It affects everyone who was involved.'

'Yes,' she said, unaware of the sadness in her tone.

He took the dish containing the syringe from her, put it on the desk and drew her into his arms. 'There'll be other happier Christmases,' he told her as he kissed her lightly on the lips.

She was grateful for his understanding and kissed him back enthusiastically. 'There's a new year round the corner,' she said.

'And there was I thinking it was next week,' he joked.

'You are a fool,' she said, laughing.

They went in to the patient together. 'Staff has an injection for you which will relieve your pain,' Scott told Duncan.

Heather administered the injection. 'Thanks, Staff,' Duncan said.

'You'll feel better soon,' she assured him with a smile.

As they left the side-ward Heather asked, 'Are you carving the turkey?'

'In the female ward,' he told her.

Scott followed her into the treatment room, where she put the used syringe into the sharps box. 'I think it would be a good idea if Michael and John have their dinner with the female patients as there's only the two of them,' Scott suggested.

'OK. If Sister Perry agrees.'

'She will if I ask her,' Scott said.

Heather looked into his blue eyes and smiled. 'I'm sure you're right,' she said cheekily. How could anyone resist him?

Scott laughed. 'You're just prejudiced.' He caught hold of her hand. 'Come on. Let's go and see the two in the ward.'

After joking with Michael and John, Scott held the door open for Heather to precede him. 'My brother wants us to come this evening for drinks,' he said. 'Will that be all right with you?'

'Yes.' She nodded.

'I'll pick you up at eight, then.'

'Right.'

The rest of the day passed quickly. The sister on the female ward agreed to Scott's suggestion. Heather remained with her solitary patient while Michael and John were having their dinner on the female ward.

Visitors came in the afternoon and stayed for tea. Michael's parents arrived, unknown to him, as a surprise, and met his girlfriend, Sandra Patterson, who was his night nurse.

John stayed in the female ward, having met a lady he had been at school with.

Staff from the other wards visited Heather, and she and David took it in turns to visit them.

Kirsty, with her arm in plaster, came to have tea with Duncan. 'Don't stay too long,' Heather advised. 'He needs to rest.'

'I won't, Heather,' she promised. 'And thanks for all you did for us last night.'

Heather just smiled.

That evening, as her green one was unwearable, Heather put on the black dress.

Scott was on time. 'Happy Christmas,' he said, handing her a parcel wrapped in Christmas paper.

He followed her into the lounge where she unwrapped the present, her eyes sparkling with anticipation. 'Scott!' she exclaimed, as her favourite perfume was revealed.

'I found, after we split up, that you were constantly in my thoughts, and I discovered I had bought the perfume absent-mindedly before I realised it,' he told her a little ruefully.

He's going to ask me for an answer now, thought Heather, hiding her anxiety behind a smile.

But Scott didn't. He just took her into his arms. 'That perfume will always remind me of you,' he said softly. 'I could never bear to buy it for someone else.' He held her closer. 'And if anything happened to you and I should smell it somewhere it would kill me,' he added with such simplicity that her eyes filled with tears.

Scott kissed her then, but it was gently. 'My darling,' he whispered, then added jauntily, after a moment to compose himself, 'And, so, where's my present?'

Heather had thought hard about what to give him and had decided that sweaters, ties and other mundane things were not good enough so she handed him an envelope.

Scott opened it and gasped. It was a paid booking for

a number of flying lessons. Heather had remembered him saying how he would like to learn. 'Darling.' He was completely astonished. 'How wonderful.' He kissed her heartily.

'You can arrange the lessons to suit yourself,' she said, happy that he liked her gift.

They left the flat and as she walked towards the car with his arm around her, as they had last night, Heather shivered a little.

His arm tightened. 'It's not going to happen tonight,' he promised.

It didn't take them long to reach Callum's flat. It was smart, expensive and very modern.

He greeted them casually at the door and took them into the lounge. The blue decor and grey furniture were too cold for Heather's liking.

Both Rosemary and Callum were smartly dressed and looked ultra-sophisticated. After greetings, and when they were settled with drinks, Rosemary said, 'What a pity you couldn't make it last evening, Scott.' She picked up a plate of canapés from the coffee-table and handed them round. 'But, then, a doctor's life isn't his own, is it?' She sounded uninterested.

'No,' answered Scott shortly.

'You must be something really special, Heather,' Callum said. 'Scott doesn't usually date nurses.' His face tightened as he looked at his brother. 'Aren't you afraid the hospital gossips will drive you to your death, like they did Mike?' His tone was brittle.

Heather was shocked, but it did explain why Scott had been so ready to fall in with her plan.

'I'm sure Heather doesn't want to hear all this,' Scott said sharply.

But Heather could see how eager Callum was to tell her, and suspected that he needed to. 'No, I'm interested in your family,' she said, taking Scott's hand and pressing it. She hoped it would take away the sudden hurt she saw in his eyes, and that he would understand her motive for what would appear to be prying.

He returned her pressure and the hurt turned to a smile. 'The conditions are not the same, Callum,' he said gently. 'And it wasn't the gossip that caused his death. He fell asleep at the wheel and was killed.'

Callum looked unconvinced.

'Tell me what happened, Callum,' Heather said gently.

'All right,' he said more quietly. Her gentleness and the compassion he saw in her eyes moved him to speak. 'Mike was a very handsome man and all the nurses were after him, but he was ambitious and not ready to settle down.' He took a sip of his drink. 'His field was gynae-cology and he was a great success with his patients.' Callum looked even more tense.

Heather could see what a strain it was to recall the details, but she didn't stop him.

'On the twenty-sixth of March last year he was taking his usual clinic. Normally a nurse was present at all times. Mike had finished seeing a patient who still had to dress. The notes for his next patient were missing so he sent the nurse to get them.'

Callum looked appealingly at Scott, who said firmly, 'You continue, Callum.' This was the first time his brother had told anyone and Scott hoped it would act as a catharsis.

'The patient was a young, attractive lady. She was small and had needed a step to climb onto the couch. As she got off the step slipped away and Mike, hearing her cry, rushed to catch her. At that moment the nurse returned and found them in what looked like a compromising position.'

A look of sadness touch Callum's eyes, which were the same blue as Scott's, as he continued, 'Mike thought no more about it until someone told him that word of his apparent misconduct was all over the hospital, spread by the nurse who had been his chaperone.

'He was furious and denied it strongly, but mud sticks.' Callum shrugged. 'He thought of suing the nurse, but didn't want the patient involved so decided to ride it out. He threw himself into his work, taking on more and more.'

Scott rose from his seat on the couch beside Heather and joined his brother, who was standing in front of the mantelpiece. He put his arm around Callum's shoulders. 'I agree,' he admitted softly. 'Mike wouldn't have driven himself so hard if that incident hadn't occurred.'

Tears filled Callum's eyes. 'I'm glad you agree at last.' He smiled and seemed surprised as he added, 'I feel like a new man.'

Heather had glanced occasionally at Rosemary while Callum was talking, and had noticed her veneer of sophistication slipping away—like an old skin being discarded—and in its place a new woman seemed to appear—a warm, loving person. Callum's catharsis had been hers also.

She rushed to Callum's side. 'Why didn't you tell me all this, my darling?' she asked in a sincere tone. 'We've wasted so much time.'

Scott handed Callum over to her welcoming arms. When Heather saw how their tears mingled as they hugged each other her own eyes became moist.

Scott put his arm round her. They collected their coats and left. In the car Scott turned to her. 'Thanks, Heather. I could never get him to talk about it, probably because I would insist that Mike's death was due to him being overtired.' Scott sighed. 'The reason I took this job was to be near Callum because I was worried he'd have a breakdown.' The concern in his eyes lifted. 'But not now,' he said cheerfully as he kissed her gently. 'And all due to you, too.'

Heather just snuggled up to him. They drove back to her flat in companionable silence. At her door he didn't accept her invitation to come in. 'I think we both need an early night.'

'Goodnight,' she said, relieved he hadn't suggested she go home with him.

CHAPTER FOURTEEN

SCOTT's loving and pleasant behaviour towards her during the following days only made Heather want to be with him for ever. She was actually longing now for him to suggest that they live together, but couldn't bring herself to voice the subject.

New Year's Eve was spent with the crowds in Princes Street, singing and watching the fireworks. As midnight boomed out Scott caught her in his arms and kissed her soundly. 'Happy New Year, my darling,' he murmured close to her ear.

'And for you with all my heart,' she whispered.

'What did you say?' he shouted above the noise of the singing and shouting crowds.

'Happy New Year to you, too,' she cried back.

Immediately those around them said, 'Thanks, and the same to you.'

Scott and Heather laughed.

After the holidays work on the ward resumed as normal. Michael was walking better. Colin came back, but was soon discharged. John left to stay with his old schoolfriend from the female ward. Duncan's recovery was slow, but visits from Kirsty helped. It was a far more mature young man who was discharged into Kirsty's care.

The panto was a great success. It was on for three days. The quips were kept reasonably within bounds as past patients had been invited with their families as well.

Len was on the door to collect the tickets. 'We've made eight hundred pounds,' he told Heather before the show on the last night.

'That's wonderful,' she exclaimed.

It had been great fun. Scott had added mischievous quips at times which had pleased the rest of the cast and made the audience hoot with laughter.

I wonder what he'll think of tonight? Heather asked herself, remembering how last night he had said as he had slipped the shoe onto her foot, 'Stafferella, you'll have to watch you don't get bunions, wearing these tight shoes.'

'No getting a laugh at my expense tonight,' she told him as they waited for the curtain to go up.

'Me?' He gave her such an innocent look that she burst out laughing.

'Shh-h,' everybody said, frowning.

Heather eyed Scott suspiciously whenever they were on stage together, but everything went well. It was at the end of the show, after he had tried on her shoe, that he said, still on bended knee, 'Will you marry me, Heather Langley?'

Heather thought he must have absent-mindedly used her real name instead of Stafferella's so, to cover up the mistake, she said gaily, 'Yes, Dr Charming, I'd love to.'

Scott drew her to her feet. 'Will you marry me, Heather?' he asked loudly, looking lovingly down into her face.

She gaped, then said, 'You're proposing?'

The audience erupted into shouts of, 'Accept him. Accept him.'

She glanced in their direction and felt their excitement adding to her own.

Scott took her into his arms. 'I want you to be my wife, Heather,' adding, so that only she could hear, 'To have and to hold for ever.'

'For ever won't be long enough,' she whispered back. It was as if they were alone.

Scott kissed her—and what a kiss! The crowd went wild, clapping, stamping and cheering.

They broke apart but he still held her hand as they bowed and the audience refused to let them go. They had to take more and more bows, but were finally allowed to leave.

The party that followed the show was turned into an engagement party, with everyone congratulating them.

They managed to sneak away eventually and fled to his flat, just as they were, still in their make-up.

Heather suddenly became shy as he led her into the lounge. 'Have a seat,' he said as he turned on the fire. 'I'll be back in a moment.'

It was quiet in the flat after the noise of the theatre. Scott returned with a tray. A bottle of champagne clinked against two glasses as he set the tray down on the coffee-table.

He handed her a glass of the bubbly liquid and sat down beside her. 'Here's to us, my darling,' Scott whispered, clinking his glass with hers. He entwined his arm with hers and they drank, upsetting the champagne slightly as they giggled.

The evening was spent discussing wedding plans. He took her into his arms and kissed her ardently. She responded with the same passion, and it was he who forced them apart. 'I think we should wait until our wedding night to make love.' He smoothed back her hair from her forehead. 'It will make it more special.'

'Oh, thank you,' she whispered, her happiness complete.

'It's very important to you, isn't it?' Scott realised it for the first time. 'And you would have given up that dream for me,' he said with sureness.

'You read minds as well?' She hoped that her joke would sweep away the self-condemnation she saw in his eyes. Her own were shining with love.

'It was seeing that young woman die that made me realise how much I needed you, not just as a partner but as a wife,' he murmured, his voice breaking with emotion. 'I don't deserve you.'

'Tell me that in few years' time when I'm driving you mad with my inconsistencies,' she said cheekily.

Scott had to laugh.

He took her home and kissed her gently goodnight.

They were married two months later in March, with Callum as Scott's best man. It was a lovely day. The wedding went smoothly, the reception was a success and the dancing afterwards enjoyable. They had asked only their close friends and relatives.

Heather's mother and father liked Scott immediately.

As Heather's uncle was leaving and they were seeing him off he said, 'I haven't given you your wedding present yet,' he said. 'Here it is.'

He handed Scott a large envelope. Scott opened it, with Heather peering over his shoulder. It was the deed to her uncle's house.

'Uncle Gavin,' she gasped.

'I know Kate would have loved you to have it. It needs

a happy couple to keep it alive and I'm sure you will be, as I was with her.' There was no sadness in his tone. 'It's too big for me and has memories round every corner so I'm buying a flat, which I shall leave to Gavin.'

Heather kissed him and Scott shook his hand. 'Thanks seem inadequate,' Scott said. 'There'll always be a room for you.'

'Thanks.'

Their honeymoon was spent in Paris. Heather gave of herself freely as he made delicious love to her. There was a lot of laughing, a lot of loving and a lot of passion between them. When dawn broke on the day after the wedding Heather lay, a complete woman, beside the man she loved.

When they arrived home they went straight to the house. Mrs Gregson, who was staying on as housekeeper, had prepared the house for their arrival before she'd gone to Canada to visit her sister for six weeks.

Scott swept Heather up into his arms and over the threshold. 'Home, Mrs McPherson,' he said, smiling down into her lovely face.

'The word has a new meaning for me now,' she told him, standing on tiptoe to kiss him.

When they went into the bedroom arm in arm that night Scott stopped suddenly.

'What's wrong?' Heather asked innocently.

'We've been taken over by ducks,' he said with a broad grin.

Side by side at the foot of the big bed were two pairs of duck slippers. 'How did you manage to get a pair big enough?' he asked as he sat down on the bed and tried on the larger size.

'I made them,' she told him as she slipped on her own.

After that their ducks played together with much laughter until Scott took her into his arms.

Later, after making love, Heather lay in his arms. 'I'll make you proud of me,' she told him a little anxiously.

He saw how vulnerable she felt. 'I *am* proud of you,' he told her sincerely. 'You're a beautiful woman, an accomplished hostess and, more importantly, you're kind, sympathetic and caring.' He kissed her gently.

'And to think that if I hadn't stepped into the road we might never have met,' she said, looking at him adoringly.

'We would have met,' he assured her softly. 'We were meant to be together and we'll be together always.'

'Always,' she whispered as he kissed her.

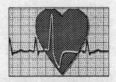

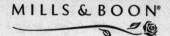

MILLS & BOON®

*Celebrate the most romantic day of the year
with a delicious collection of short stories...*

VALENTINE DELIGHTS

A matchmaking shop owner dispenses sinful desserts,
mouth-watering chocolates...and advice to the
lovelorn, in this collection of three delightfully
romantic stories by Meryl Sawyer, Kate Hoffmann
and Gina Wilkins.

Plus FREE chocolate for every reader!
see book for details

Available: January 1998

4 FREE

books and a surprise gift!

We would like to take this opportunity to thank you for reading this Mills & Boon® book by offering you the chance to take FOUR more specially selected titles from the Medical Romance™ series absolutely FREE! We're also making this offer to introduce you to the benefits of the Reader Service™—

- ★ FREE home delivery
- ★ FREE gifts and competitions
- ★ FREE monthly newsletter
- ★ Books available before they're in the shops
- ★ Exclusive Reader Service discounts

Accepting these FREE books and gift places you under no obligation to buy, you may cancel at any time, even after receiving your free shipment. Simply complete your details below and return the entire page to the address below. *You don't even need a stamp!*

YES! Please send me 4 free Medical Romance books and a surprise gift. I understand that unless you hear from me, I will receive 4 superb new titles every month for just £2.20 each, postage and packing free. I am under no obligation to purchase any books and may cancel my subscription at any time. The free books and gift will be mine to keep in any case.

M8XE

Ms/Mrs/Miss/Mr ....Initials ....
BLOCK CAPITALS PLEASE

Surname ....

Address ....

....

....Postcode................................

Send this whole page to:
The Reader Service, Freepost, Croydon, CR9 3WZ
(Eire readers please send coupon to: P.O. Box 4546, Dublin 24.)

Offer not valid to current Reader Service subscribers to this series. We reserve the right to refuse an application and applicants must be aged 18 years or over. Only one application per household. Terms and prices subject to change without notice. Offer expires 31st July 1998. You may be mailed with offers from other reputable companies as a result of this application. If you would prefer not to receive such offers, please tick box. ☐

Mills & Boon® Medical Romance™ is a registered trademark of Harlequin Mills & Boon Ltd.

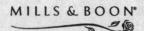